John Ford's Perkin Warbeck: A Retelling

David Bruce

Published by David Bruce, 2022.

This is a work of fiction. Similarities to real people, places, or events are entirely coincidental.

JOHN FORD'S PERKIN WARBECK: A RETELLING

First edition. July 9, 2022.

Copyright © 2022 David Bruce.

ISBN: 979-8201690922

Written by David Bruce.

Table of Contents

Dedication

Dedicated to Carl Eugene Bruce and Josephine Saturday Bruce

My father, Carl Eugene Bruce, died on 24 October 2013. He used to work for Ohio Power, and at one time, his job was to shut off the electricity of people who had not paid their bills. He sometimes would find a home with an impoverished mother and some children. Instead of shutting off their electricity, he would tell the mother that she needed to pay her bill or soon her electricity would be shut off. He would write on a form that no one was home when he stopped by because if no one was home he did not have to shut off their electricity.

The best good deed that anyone ever did for my father occurred after a storm that knocked down many power lines. He and other linemen worked long hours and got wet and cold. Their feet were freezing because water got into their boots and soaked their socks. Fortunately, a kind woman gave my father and the other linemen dry socks to wear.

My mother, Josephine Saturday Bruce, died on 14 June 2003. She used to work at a store that sold clothing. One day, an impoverished mother with a baby clothed in rags walked into the store and started shoplifting in an interesting way: The mother took the rags off her baby and dressed the infant in new clothing. My mother knew that this mother could not afford to buy the clothing, but she helped the mother dress her baby and then she watched as the mother walked out of the store without paying.

***

The doing of good deeds is important. As a free person, you can choose to live your life as a good person or as a bad person. To be a good person, do good deeds. To be a bad person, do bad deeds. If you do good deeds, you will become good. If you do bad deeds, you will become bad. To become the person you want to be, act as if you already are that kind of person. Each of us chooses what kind of person we will become. To become a good person, do the things a good person does. To become a bad person, do the things a bad person does. The opportunity to take action to become the kind of person you want to be is yours.

Human beings have free will. According to the Babylonian Niddah 16b, whenever a baby is to be conceived, the Lailah (angel in charge of contraception) takes the drop of semen that will result in the conception and asks God, "Sovereign of the Universe, what is going to be the fate of this drop? Will it develop into a robust or into a weak person? An intelligent or a stupid person? A wealthy or a poor person?" The Lailah asks all these questions, but it does not ask, "Will it develop into a righteous or a wicked person?" The answer to that question lies in the decisions to be freely made by the human being that is the result of the conception.

A Buddhist monk visiting a class wrote this on the chalkboard: "EVERYONE WANTS TO SAVE THE WORLD, BUT NO ONE WANTS TO HELP MOM DO THE DISHES." The students laughed, but the monk then said, "Statistically, it's highly unlikely that any of you will ever have the opportunity to run into a burning orphanage and rescue an infant. But, in the smallest gesture of kindness — a warm smile, holding the door for the person behind you, shoveling the driveway of the elderly person next door — you have committed an act of immeasurable profundity, because to each of us, our life is our universe."

Cover Photo for John Ford's *Perkin Warbeck*: A Retelling: https://pixabay.com/photos/man-people-face-shadow-sadness-315906/

***

According to Charles Lamb, "Ford was of the first order of poets. He sought for sublimity, not by parcels in metaphors or visible images, but directly where she has her full residence in the heart of man; in the actions and sufferings of the greatest minds."

Educate Yourself
Read Like A Wolf Eats
Books Then, Books Now, Books Forever
Be Excellent to Each Other

❧❧❧

In this retelling, as in all my retellings, I have tried to make the work of literature accessible to modern readers who may lack some of the knowledge about mythology, religion, and history that the literary work's contemporary audience had.

Do you know a language other than English? If you do, I give you permission to translate this book, copyright your translation, publish or self-publish it, and keep all the royalties for yourself. (Do give me credit, of course, for the original retelling.)

I would like to see my retellings of classic literature used in schools, so I give permission to the country of Finland (and all other countries) to give copies of any or all of my retellings to all students forever. I also give permission to the state of Texas (and all other states) to give copies of any or all of my retellings to all students forever. I also give permission to all teachers to give copies of any or all of my retellings to all students forever. Of course, libraries are welcome to use my eBooks for free.

Teachers need not actually teach my retellings. Teachers are welcome to give students copies of my eBooks as background material. For example, if they are teaching Homer's *Iliad* and *Odyssey*, teachers are welcome to give students copies of my *Virgil's* Aeneid: *A Retelling in Prose* and tell them, "Here's another ancient epic you may want to read in your spare time.

CAST OF CHARACTERS

THE ENGLISH

Henry VII, King of England.

Lord Giles Dawbeney.

Sir William Stanley, Lord Chamberlain (the chief officer of the royal household).

Earl of Oxford.

Earl of Surrey.

Richard Fox, Bishop of Durham.

Christopher Urswick, Chaplain to King Henry VII.

Sir Robert Clifford.

Lambert Simnel.

Pedro Hialas, a Spanish Ambassador for Ferdinand and Isabella of Spain. On the side of King Henry VII.

***

THE SCOTTISH

James IV, King of Scotland.

Earl of Huntley.

Lady Katherine Gordon, his Daughter.

Jane Douglas, Lady Katherine's Attendant.

Earl of Crawford.

Countess of Crawford, his Wife.

Lord Dalyell.

Marchmont, a Herald.

***

THE REBELS

Perkin Warbeck.

Warbeck's followers:

• *Stephen Frion*, his secretary.

• *John a-Water*, Mayor of Cork, Ireland, in 1490 and 1494.

• *John Heron*, a Mercer, aka a Dealer in Textile Fabrics.
• *Edward Skelton*, a Tailor.
• *Nicholas Astley*, a Scrivener, aka a Legal Clerk. As a Scrivener, he copied legal documents.

***

MINOR CHARACTERS

Sheriff, Constable, Officers, Messenger, Guards, Soldiers, Masquers, and Attendants.

***

SCENE

Partly in England, and partly in Scotland.

***

NOTES

The full title of John Ford's play is *The Chronicle History of Perkin Warbeck: A Strange Truth*. It was first acted in 1633.

When King Richard III fell at the Battle of Bosworth, Henry Tudor, Earl of Richmond, became King Henry VII (reigned 1485-1509). A Lancastrian, he married Elizabeth of York — young Elizabeth of York in William Shakespeare's *Richard III* — and united the two warring houses, York and Lancaster, thus ending the Wars of the Roses. His reign was troubled because many Pretenders to the throne, including Lambert Simnel and Perkin Warbeck, appeared.

Perkin Warbeck (born 1474, died 23 November 1499) was a Fleming (born in Tournai, Belgium) who claimed to be Richard of Shrewsbury, Duke of York, who was the second son of King Edward IV. Richard of Shrewsbury was one of the two Princes in the Tower of London who may have been murdered (in 1483) so that Richard, Duke of Gloucester, could become King Richard III. Richard of Shrewsbury, Duke of York, if still alive, would have been the rightful claimant to the throne if his elder brother King Edward V were dead.

John Ford's play begins in 1495, when Perkin Warbeck was gaining support for his claim to the throne of England.

Margaret of Burgundy — the sister of King Edward IV and of King Richard III — helped train Perkin Warbeck to appear to be aristocratic and supported his attempt to become King of England.

Before this play begins, Lambert Simnel had claimed to be Edward, Earl of Warwick, the nephew of King Edward IV and the son of Edward IV's brother George, Earl of Clarence. The Earl of Warwick was still alive and imprisoned in the Tower of London by order of King Henry VII, but he would be beheaded on 28 November 1499.

In the Prologue of this play, John Ford states that he does not introduce unnecessary comic scenes in an attempt to be popular.

In the Prologue of this play, John Ford states that by writing this play, he is trying to make popular again the kind of history plays that William Shakespeare used to write.

In the Prologue of this play, John Ford states that he attempts to be both truthful and dramatic.

In this culture, a man of higher rank would use words such as "thee," "thy," "thine," and "thou" to refer to a servant. However, two close friends or a husband and wife could properly use "thee," "thy," "thine," and "thou" to refer to each other.

The word "sirrah" is a term usually used to address a man of lower social rank than the speaker. This was socially acceptable, but sometimes the speaker would use the word as an insult when speaking to a man whom he did not usually call "sirrah."

The word "House," as in House of York or House of Lancaster, means "Family."

In Act 2 Scene 3, the Earl of Huntley calls himself "Alexander" one time, but his name was actually George Gordon, and he was the second Earl of Huntley. He died in 1524. The error in name appeared in some of John Ford's sources.

As is frequent in historical plays of William Shakespeare's time, the historical timeline is altered for dramatic reasons. These are the correct times:

• Sir William Stanley — the Lord Chamberlain — was convicted of treason on 6 February 1495 in a trial by his peers. He was executed on 16 February 1495.

• In November of 1495, King James IV of Scotland received Perkin Warbeck. (John Ford incorrectly has Sir William Stanley's trial and death occurring after Perkin Warbeck was well received by King James IV of Scotland.)

• The Scottish invasion into England took place in 1496.

• The Cornish rebellion took place in late spring of 1497. (John Ford incorrectly has the Cornish invasion occurring before the Scottish invasion of 1496.)

• The Battle of Blackheath, aka the Battle of Deptford Bridge, took place on 17 June 1497.

• In history, Perkin Warbeck confessed to being an imposter. In this play, he never confesses to that and he may believe that he really is the Duke of York.

PROLOGUE

Studies have of this nature been of late
    So out of fashion, so unfollowed, that
    It is become more justice to revive
    The antic follies of the times than strive
    To countenance wise industry. No want
    Of art doth render wit or lame or scant
    Or slothful in the purchase of fresh bays;
    But want of truth in them who give the praise
    To their self-love, presuming to out-do
    The writer, or, for need, the actors, too.
    But such This Author's silence best befits,
    Who bids them be in love with their own wits.
    From him to clearer judgments, we can say,
    He shows a history couched in a play,
    A history of noble mention, known,
    Famous, and true: most noble, 'cause our own:
    Not forged from Italy, from France, from Spain,
    But chronicled at home; as rich in strain
    Of brave attempts as ever fertile rage
    In action could beget to grace the stage.
    We cannot limit scenes, for the whole land
    Itself appeared too narrow to withstand
    Competitors for kingdoms: nor is here
    Unnecessary mirth forced, to endear
    A multitude; on these two, rests the fate
    Of worthy expectation: Truth and State.

***

This is the Prologue in Modern English:
    Plays of this nature have been recently so out of fashion and so unfollowed [since William Shakespeare's HENRY VIII (1613)] that it has become more

judicious and more sensible to revive the grotesque follies of the times than strive to look favorably on wise industry.

No lack of art renders wit and intelligence either lame or scant or slothful in the purchase of fresh bay (laurel) garlands of distinction for poets, but lack of truth in them who give the praise to their own self-love, presuming to out-do the writer, or, if necessary, the actors, too.

But such people this author's — John Ford's — silence best befits, for John Ford tells them to be in love with their own wits.

John Ford to clearer judgments, we can say, shows a history [Francis Bacon's *History of the Reign of King Henry VII* (1622)] expressed in a play, a history of noble record, known, famous, and true: It is most noble because it is our own. It is not fashioned from Italy, from France, or from Spain, but is chronicled at home in our England, and it is as rich in ancestral line of brave attempts as always fertile strong emotion in performance could beget to grace the stage.

We cannot limit scenes to any one particular place, for the whole land itself appeared too narrow to withstand competitors for kingdoms, nor is here unnecessary mirth forced in order to endear and attract a multitude; the fate of worthy expectation rests on these two: Truth and State.

Note: By State is meant Matter of State, and Stateliness.

CHAPTER 1

— 1.1 —

King Henry VII entered the royal Presence Chamber in the King's palace at Westminster. The Bishop of Durham and Sir William Stanley (the Lord Chamberlain) followed him as he walked to the throne. The Earl of Oxford, the Earl of Surrey, Lord Giles Dawbeney, and some guards were also present.

King Henry VII began to complain about the Pretenders to the throne — they were disrupting the country.

The year was 1495, and the Pretender Perkin Warbeck was gaining support for his claim to the throne of England. Previously, the Pretender Lambert Simnel had caused trouble for King Henry VII.

King Henry VII said, "Always to be haunted, always to be pursued, always to be frightened with false apparitions of pageant — mimic — majesty and new-coined greatness, as if we were a mockery, counterfeit King in state, only ordained to lavish sweat and blood, in scorn and laughter, to the ghosts of York, is all below our merits — I don't deserve this trouble!"

Richard, the third Duke of York, was the father of King Edward IV and King Richard III and of the Earl of Clarence. The "ghosts of York" were the various Pretenders to the throne — Pretenders who falsely claimed to be descendants of Richard, the third Duke of York. These Pretenders included Lambert Simnel and Perkin Warbeck.

Using the royal plural, and comparing himself to a physician, King Henry VII said, "Yet, my lords, my friends and counselors, yet we sit fast in our own royal birthright; the rent face and bleeding wounds of England's slaughtered people have been by us, as if by the best physician, at last both thoroughly cured and set in safety; and yet, for all this glorious work of peace, ourselves is scarcely secure."

"Ourselves is" meant "I am." He was using the royal plural.

"The rage of malice and hatred conjures fresh spirits with the spells of York," the Bishop of Durham said. "For ninety years ten English Kings and princes, threescore great dukes and earls, a thousand lords and valiant knights, and two hundred fifty thousand English subjects have in civil wars been sacrificed to an uncivil thirst of discord and ambition."

Long had England been unquiet. In 1399, Henry Bolingbroke usurped the crown from King Richard II and became King Henry IV. The Hundred Years' War with France took place from 1337 to 1453. From 1455-1487, the Yorkists and the Lancastrians fought for power in England in the Wars of the Roses. In 1485, King Henry VII was crowned after the Yorkist King Richard III was killed in the Battle of Bosworth, but King Henry VII still had to fight for a couple of years more. In 1486, King Henry VII, who was a Lancastrian, married Elizabeth of York, thus uniting the two families. Unfortunately, Pretenders to the throne, claiming to be Yorkists, troubled his reign.

The Bishop of Durham said to King Henry VII, "This hot vengeance of the just powers above — Providence — to utter ruin and desolation would have continued to rain on, except that Mercy did gently sheathe the sword of Justice and lent to this blood-drained — because of war — and therefore withered commonwealth a new soul and a new birth in your sacred person."

Lord Giles Dawbeney said, "King Edward IV, after a fearful fortune, yielded his life to nature, leaving to his sons, Edward and Richard, the inheritance of a most bloody acquisition — instead of inheriting his crown, King Edward IV acquired it by usurping it from King Henry VI. Richard the tyrant, their unnatural uncle, forced these two young princes to a violent grave."

"Richard the tyrant" was King Richard III, but Lord Giles Dawbeney and the others present would not refer to him as "King" because they did not want to seem to be conferring legitimacy to his title.

King Edward IV had left behind two sons: Edward (born 1470), who reigned briefly as King Edward V, and Richard, Duke of York (born 1473). The two boys disappeared while in the Tower of London in 1483. Many people believed that Richard, Duke of Gloucester, had ordered that they be murdered so that he could become King Richard III.

King Richard III was the "unnatural" uncle of King Edward IV's two sons — Edward and Richard — because he had ordered that these nephews be murdered — so people believed.

Lord Giles Dawbeney continued, "So just is Heaven that your majesty by your own arm, divinely strengthened, pulled Richard the tyrant from his boar's sty, and struck the black usurper to a carcass."

King Richard III's personal device — emblematic figure — was the White Boar.

Lord Giles Dawbeney continued, "Nor does the House of York decay in honors, although Lancaster does repossess his right, for King Edward IV's daughter — Elizabeth of York — is King Henry VII's queen."

When King Richard III fell at the Battle of Bosworth, Henry Tudor, Earl of Richmond, became King Henry VII (reigned 1485-1509). A Lancastrian, he married Elizabeth of York — young Elizabeth of York in William Shakespeare's *Richard III* — and united the two warring families, York and Lancaster, thus effectively ending the Wars of the Roses. (The last major battle of the Wars of the Roses was the Battle of Stoke Field on 16 June 1487.) Despite this marriage, many Pretenders to the throne, including Lambert Simnel and Perkin Warbeck, appeared.

King Henry VII was the first Tudor King of England.

Lord Giles Dawbeney continued, "This is a blessed union, and a lasting blessing for this poor panting island, if some shreds, some useless remnant of the House of York would not begrudge this happiness and blessing."

The shreds — the useless remnant of the House of York — were the Pretenders to the throne.

The Earl of Oxford said, "Margaret of Burgundy — the sister of King Edward IV and of Richard the tyrant — blows fresh coals of division."

Margaret of Burgundy, a Yorkist, supported the Pretenders' claims to the throne of England. She had supported Lambert Simnel, and now she supported Perkin Warbeck.

The Earl of Surrey said, "These fresh coals of division are painted, artificial fires, without either heat to scorch or light to cherish."

Lord Giles Dawbeney said, "Neither the headless trunk of the Duke of York, Margaret's father, who was killed in the Battle of Wakefield in 1460; nor the fate of King Edward IV, her brother; nor the smothering of her nephews by the tyrant Richard of Gloucester, brother to her nature; nor Richard of Gloucester's own destruction — all decrees sacred in Heaven — can move this woman-monster. She still, from the bottomless mine of devilish policies, vents and discharges the ore of troubles and sedition."

The tyrant Richard of Gloucester was King Richard III, who was the Duke of Gloucester before becoming King of England.

King Henry VII and his supporters never referred to Duke Richard of Gloucester as King Richard III.

The Earl of Oxford said, "In her age — great sir, observe the wonder — she grows fruitful, although in her strength of youth she was always barren. Nor are her births as other mothers' are that end after nine or ten months; she has been pregnant eight years, or seven years at least. When her 'twins' were born — a monstrosity in nature — even the youngest was fifteen years of age at his first entrance, as soon as he became known in the world. They are tall striplings, strong and able to give battle to Kings; they are idols of Yorkish malice."

The "twins" were two Pretenders to the throne of England: Lambert Simnel and Perkin Warbeck. The Earl of Oxford was mocking Margaret of Burgundy. Although she was past the age of child-bearing, yet she was producing "children" — the two Pretenders.

Lord Giles Dawbeney said, "And they are only idols. A steely hammer — King Henry VII — crushes them to pieces."

King Henry VII said, "Lambert Simnel, the eldest, lords, is in our service, promoted from the scullery to a falconer because of his zealous and eager-to-serve disposition — a strange precedent! Such a promotion shows the difference between noble natures and the base-born."

Lambert Simnel had claimed to be Edward, Earl of Warwick, the son of King Edward IV's brother George, Earl of Clarence. In 1487, Lambert Simnel and his supporters crossed from Ireland to England, but King Henry VII decisively defeated their army. He pardoned Lambert Simnel and gave him a job in the royal kitchens but later promoted him to falconer. King Henry VII considered this a strange precedent because a person with a noble nature would be expected to rise, but Lambert Simnel's history as a Pretender showed that he had an ignoble nature and so would be expected to continue serving in the King's kitchens.

King Henry VII continued, "But as for the upstart and newly revived Duke of York, Edward's second son, murdered long ago in the Tower of London — he lives again and vows to be your King."

The upstart Duke was Perkin Warbeck, who claimed to be Richard of Shrewsbury, Duke of York, who was the second son of King Edward IV. He and his brother had disappeared while imprisoned in the Tower of London; people presumed that Richard of Gloucester had had them murdered so he could become King Richard III.

"The throne is filled, sir," Sir William Stanley said.

"True, Stanley," King Henry VII said, "and I, the lawful heir, sit on it. A guard of angels and the holy prayers of loyal subjects are a sure defense against all invasion of open force and all secret plans of invasion.

"But now, my lords, let us suppose that some of our nobles, our 'great ones,' should give support and courage to 'pretty' 'Duke' Perkin Warbeck. You will all confess that our generous bounties have been unthriftily and unprofitably scattered among unthankful men."

Some of the people whom King Henry VII had pardoned or favored were being disloyal to him.

"They are unthankful beasts, dogs, villains, traitors!" Lord Giles Dawbeney said.

"Giles Dawbeney, let the guilty keep silence," King Henry VII said. "I accuse none, although I know that foreign attempts against a state and kingdom are seldom without some great friends at home."

Sir William Stanley said, "Sir, even if no other abler reasons than duty or allegiance could divert a headstrong resolution, yet the dangers so lately experienced by men of high birth and fortunes in Lambert Simnel's party must command more than a fear — they must command a terror — to conspirators.

"Consider the high-born Earl of Lincoln (son to De la Pole), the Earl of Kildare, the Lord Geraldine, Francis Lord Lovell, and the bold German baron Martin Swart, along with Sir Thomas Broughton and the rest — most are spectacles of ruin, but some are spectacles of mercy, for some were executed, and some were pardoned. But all of them are precedents sufficient to forewarn the present times, or any who live in them, about what folly, indeed, what madness, it would be to lift a finger up in any cause but yours — defending any cause but yours must necessarily be fraudulent. You are the only true King of England."

The men whom Sir William Stanley had mentioned were supporters of Lambert Simnel.

King Richard III had been killed in 1485, but because of Pretenders such as Lambert Simnel, King Henry VII still had to fight to keep his hold on the throne.

John De la Pole, the Earl of Lincoln, was killed at the Battle of Stoke Field on 16 June 1487. The Battle of Stoke Field was the last major battle of the Wars of the Roses; it was fought in an attempt to make Lambert Simnel the King of England.

The Earl of Kildare was pardoned by King Henry VII.

Thomas Lord Geraldine was killed at the Battle of Stoke Field.

Francis Lovell, Viscount, disappeared.

Martin Schwartz, who led 1500 mercenaries sent by Margaret of Burgundy to support the Yorkists, was killed at the Battle of Stoke Field.

Sir Thomas Broughton disappeared.

King Henry VII said, "Stanley, we know thou love us, and thy heart is portrayed on thy tongue — you speak what is in your heart — nor do we think less of any who is here."

He said to the nobles present, "How closely we have hunted this cub from hole to hole, since he left his lair, your knowledge is our chronicle — you know the history of how we have hunted Perkin Warbeck.

"First Ireland, the common stage of new thought and common source of rebellion, presented this gewgaw — this person of no value — to oppose us. In Ireland the Geraldine family and the Butler family, both of whom supported Lambert Simnell, once again stood in support of this colossic statue named Perkin Warbeck."

A colossic statue is impressive on the outside, but not on the inside. George Chapman wrote in his tragedy *Bussy d'Amboise*, "those colossic statues, / Which with heroic forms, without o'erspread, / Within are nought [nothing] but mortar, flint, and lead."

King Henry VII continued, "King Charles VIII of France thence called Perkin Warbeck into his protection and pretended that he was the lawful heir of England — yet this was all only French dissimulation, aiming at peace with us. Once this peace was granted on honorable terms on our part with the Treaty of Étaples in 1492, suddenly this smoke of straw — Perkin Warbeck — was sent packing from France again, to infect some grosser air: and now we learn — in spite of the malice of Sir George Neville the Bastard, Sir John Taylor, and a hundred English rebels who joined Perkin Warbeck in Paris — that they've all retired to Flanders, to the dam — the mother — that nursed this eager whelp, Margaret of Burgundy. But we will hunt him there, too; we will hunt him. We will hunt him to death, even in the beldam's — the old woman's — private chamber, and we will hunt him to death even if the Archduke Maximilian of Austria were his shield!"

After living for part of 1491 in Ireland, Perkin Warbeck arrived in France in October 1492 as the invited guest of King Charles VIII of France. King Henry VII invaded and besieged Boulogne. The two Kings made peace with the Treaty of Étaples in November 1492, and Perkin Warbeck was forced to leave France. He went to Flanders, where Margaret of Burgundy hosted him.

The Earl of Surrey said, "Margaret of Burgundy has given Perkin Warbeck the title 'The Fair White Rose of England.'"

In the Wars of the Roses, the emblem of the Yorkists was the white rose, while the emblem of the Lancastrians was the red rose. Margaret of Burgundy was a Yorkist, while King Henry VII was a Lancastrian.

Lord Giles Dawbeney said, "Perkin Warbeck a jolly gentleman? He is more suitable to be a swabber — a sailor who mops the decks of boats — to the Flemish after a drunken excess."

According to Lord Giles Dawbeney, Perkin Warbeck was the type of person to get shanghaied to serve as a sailor after getting thoroughly drunk.

Carrying a paper, Christopher Urswick, King Henry VII's chaplain, entered the scene and said to King Henry VII, "Gracious sovereign, may it please you to peruse this paper."

King Henry VII took the paper and began to read it.

Watching him, the Bishop of Durham said quietly, "The King's countenance gathers a sprightly blood."

"It is good news," Lord Giles Dawbeney said. "You may believe it."

"Christopher Urswick, lend me thine ear," King Henry VII said. "Listen to me. Have thou lodged him? Have you given him a place to stay?"

"Him" was Sir Robert Clifford, who had joined King Henry VII's side after supporting Perkin Warbeck.

"He is strongly safe, sir," Christopher Urswick said. "He is secure."

"Enough," King Henry VII said. "Has William Barley come, too?"

William Barley had not come because he was still loyal to the Yorkists who supported Perkin Warbeck.

Earlier, both Sir Robert Clifford and William Barley had visited Perkin Warbeck in Flanders. King Henry VII had offered both Sir Robert Clifford and William Barley pardons if they would join his side and inform on those opposing him. Sir Robert Clifford immediately accepted the pardon, but William Barley remained opposed to King Henry VII and loyal to Perkin Warbeck for a few more years.

"No, my lord," Christopher Urswick replied.

"It doesn't matter," King Henry VII said. "Phew! He's only a spreading weed that will be plucked up by the roots when I please. But I will say more about this soon."

He then said to the lords who were present, "I have decided, my lords, for reasons that you shall share, that it is our pleasure to move our court from Westminster to the Tower of London."

The Tower of London had quarters for the King and his retinue. It also served as a prison for nobles.

King Henry VII continued, "We will lodge this very night there."

He ordered, "Give, Lord Chamberlain, an immediate order for it."

Sir William Stanley, who was the Lord Chamberlain, thought, *The Tower of London!*

He then replied to King Henry VII, "I shall, sir."

"Come, my true, best, fast friends," King Henry VII said. "These clouds will vanish, the sun will shine at full, the heavens are clearing."

— 1.2 —

The Earl of Huntley and Lord Dalyell talked together in an apartment in the Earl of Huntley's house in Edinburgh, Scotland. Lord Dalyell wanted permission to court Lady Elizabeth, the Earl of Huntley's daughter.

"You are wasting your time, sir," the Earl of Huntley said.

"Oh, my noble lord," Lord Dalyell said, "you construe my griefs to so hard and unfeeling a sense that where the text provides evidence that deserves pity, being a matter of earnest love, your interpretation corrupts it with too much ill-placed mirth."

"Much mirth!" the Earl of Huntley said. "Lord Dalyell! That is not so, I vow. Observe me, thou sprightly gallant. I know thou are a noble and handsome lad, descended from an honorable ancestry. I know that thou are spirited and active, and that you resolve to wrestle and do battle in the world by doing noble deeds so that you are splendidly remembered by posterity."

"I don't scorn thy affection for my daughter, not I, by good Saint Andrew — Scotland's patron saint. But this bugbear, this whoreson tale of honor —

14

honor, Dalyell! — so hourly chats and tattles in my ear about the piece of royalty that is stitched-up in my Kate's blood that it is as dangerous for thee, young lord, to perch so near an eaglet as foolish for a man of my gravity and social standing to allow it: I have spoken all at once — I have said what necessity required me to say."

Lord Dalyell wanted to marry Lady Katherine, the Earl of Huntley's daughter, but Dalyell, although he was a lord, lacked royal blood. The Earl of Huntley's wife, Annabella, was the daughter of King James I of Scotland, and therefore Lady Katherine had royal blood and so was expected to marry someone of her own social class. Lord Dalyell was too far below Lady Katherine's social class to marry her, although in all other respects he was qualified and the Earl of Huntley would welcome him as a son-in-law.

"Sir, with this truth you mix such bitter wormwood that you leave no hope for my disordered palate ever to relish a wholesome taste again," Lord Dalyell replied. "Alas, I know, sir, what an unequal distance lies between great Huntley's daughter's birth and Dalyell's fortunes. She's the King's kinswoman, placed near the crown, a princess of the blood, and I am a subject."

"Right, but you are a noble subject," the Earl of Huntley said. "Don't neglect to mention that."

"I could add more," Lord Dalyell replied. "In the rightest line I derive my pedigree from Adam Mure, a Scottish knight whose daughter was the mother to him who first begot the race of Jameses, who sway the scepter to this very day."

He was connecting his genealogy to Scottish royalty, going from the Scottish knight Adam Muir to King James I of Scotland and his descendants.

Adam Muir's daughter Elizabeth married the High Steward of Scotland. Elizabeth died before 1355, and the High Steward became King Robert II of Scotland in 1370. The son of Elizabeth and Robert was born in 1337, and he became King Robert III of Scotland. King Robert III's son became King James I of Scotland, who ruled from 1406 to 1437.

He continued, "But lineages are not ours when once the period of many years have swallowed up the memory of their originals. Similarly, pasture-fields neighboring too near the ocean are swept up and swallowed and known no more. If I stood in my first and native greatness, and had the social status that my ancestors had, then if the princely woman I love — your daughter — would not acknowledge me as her servant who loves her, it would be as good to me to be nothing, as to be raised to a throne of wonder."

The Earl of Huntley thought, *Now, by Saint Andrew, he is a spark of mettle! He is a gallant young man, and he has a brave fire in him: I wish that he would marry my daughter, as long as I didn't know that they were married. But it must not be so — it must not.*

He said out loud, "Well, young lord, this will not do. Yet, if the girl were to be headstrong and not listen to good counsel and advice, then steal her and run away with her; dance lively galliards, do, and frisk about the world to learn the languages. It will be a thriving trade; you may set up by it."

"Set up" meant "set up housekeeping" and possibly "set up a business."

He was advising Lord Dalyell to run away with Elizabeth and travel the world outside of Scotland.

"Begging your pardon, noble Gordon, this disdain does not suit your daughter's virtue or my constancy," Lord Dalyell said.

The Earl of Huntley's family name was Gordon.

"You're angry," the Earl of Huntley said.

He thought, *I wish he would beat me; I deserve it.*

He then said out loud, "Dalyell, give me thy hand; we're friends. Pursue thy courtship of my daughter. Take thine own time and speak to her about marriage. If thou prevail more with her with thine passion than I can with my counsel, then she's thine. Indeed, she is thine — it is a fair match, free and allowed.

"I'll use only my tongue when advising her to marry someone of her own social status, and I will not use a father's power and force her not to marry thee. Use thine tongue and persuade her to marry you."

The Earl of Huntley was telling Lord Dalyell that he would tell Elizabeth not to marry him, but that he would not force her not to marry him. If Lord Dalyell could convince Elizabeth to marry him, then he could marry her.

The Earl of Huntley continued with some proverbs: "Self do, self have; no more words; win her and wear her."

"You bless me," Lord Dalyell said. "I am now too poor in thanks to pay the debt I owe you."

The Earl of Huntley said, "Nay, thou are poor enough."

Lord Dalyell may have lacked wealth.

The Earl of Huntley thought about Lord Dalyell, *I love his spirit infinitely.*

He then said, "Look, she is coming. To her now, to her, to her!"

"To her!" meant "Woo her strongly!"

Lady Katherine and Jane Douglas, her attendant, entered the room.

Lady Katherine said to her father, the Earl of Huntley, "The King commands your presence, sir."

The King was James IV, King of Scotland.

The Earl of Huntley replied, "The gallant" — he motioned toward Lord Dalyell — "this, this, this lord, this servant, Kate, of yours, desires to be your master."

A "servant" could be a wooer, a devotee, or a lover. A "master" in this context was a husband.

"I acknowledge him to be a worthy friend of mine," Lady Katherine replied.

A "friend" could be a well-wisher, a wooer, or a lover.

"I am your humblest creature," Lord Dalyell said to Lady Katherine.

The Earl of Huntley thought, *So! So! The game's a-foot. I'm in cold hunting and have lost the scent. The hare and hounds are parties who are on the same side: They are partners.*

The Earl of Huntley suspected that the wooing process had begun earlier and was more advanced than he had thought.

Lord Dalyell said to Lady Katherine, "Princely lady, how most unworthy I am to employ my services in honor of your virtues, how hopeless my desires are to enjoy your fair opinion, and much more your love, are only matter of despair, unless your goodness will give large warrant to my boldness, my feeble-winged ambition."

The Earl of Huntley thought, *This is scurvy.*

He wanted the Lord Dalyell's wooing of Lady Katherine to be less stilted and less formal and less fawning.

Lord Dalyell paused and Lady Katherine said, "My lord, I am not interrupting you."

The Earl of Huntley thought, *Indeed! Now, on my life, she'll court him.*

He believed that Elizabeth would make a better wooer than Lord Dalyell.

He said to Lord Dalyell, "Go on, sir."

Lord Dalyell said to Lady Katherine, "Often have I tuned my sorrows as if they were a musical instrument to sweeten discord and enrich your pity and sympathy for me, but all in vain — here my comforts would have sunk, and never risen again to tell a story of the despairing lover, had not now, even now, the Earl your father —"

The Earl of Huntley thought, *He means me, surely.*

Lord Dalyell continued, "— after some appropriate statements concerning your social rank, your highness and my lowness, has given me license and permission to woo you that did not more embolden than encourage my faulting tongue."

It was true that the Earl of Huntley had encouraged Lord Dalyell to court Elizabeth, but the Earl of Huntley had wanted Lord Dalyell to keep that secret.

The Earl of Huntley said, "What! What! What's that! Embolden! Encourage! I encourage you! Do you hear me, sir?"

He thought, *That was a subtle trick, an ingenious one.*

Lord Dalyell had let Lady Katherine know that her father supported his wooing of her.

The Earl of Huntley continued, "Will you hear me, man? What did I say to you? Come, come, to the point."

"It is not necessary to hear that, my lord," Lady Katherine said to her father.

The Earl of Huntley said, "Then listen to me, Kate."

He said to Lord Dalyell, "Keep on that side of her; I will be on this side."

He then said to Lady Katherine, "Thou stand between a father and a suitor, both striving for an interest in thy heart.

"He courts thee for affection, I for duty.

"He as a wooer pleads, but although I by the privilege of nature might command you to obey my wishes as a father, yet my loving concern for you shall only counsel what it shall not force.

"Thou can make only one choice: The ties of marriage cannot be broken at will, but will last during all thine life.

"Consider whose thou are, and who: a princess — a princess of the royal blood of Scotland, in the full spring of youth and fresh in beauty.

"The King who sits upon the throne is young and as yet unmarried, and he is too eager to engage in endeavors on any least occasion that do endanger his person."

It was possible for Lady Katherine to marry the young King James IV of Scotland, but the Earl of Huntley carefully mentioned a reason for why his daughter might not want to marry him. His recklessness could make her a young widow.

The Earl of Huntley continued, "Wherefore, Kate, as I am confident thou dare not wrong thy birth and education by yielding to a common servile, slave-like passion of female wantonness, so I am confident thou will proportion all thy thoughts to match thy equals, if not equal thy superiors.

"My Lord of Dalyell, young in years, is old in honors, but he is neither eminent in titles nor in estate that may support or add to the expectation of thy fortunes. Settle thy will and reason by a strength of judgment, for, in a word, I give thee freedom — take it. If impartial fates have not ordained to pitch thy hopes above my height, then don't let thy passion lead thee to shrink my honor in oblivion.

"Thou are thine own person. I have finished speaking."

The Earl of Huntley had made it clear that his daughter was free to decide whom to marry, although he had also fulfilled societal expectations by advising her not to marry below her social standing.

Lord Dalyell said to the Earl of Huntley, "Oh, you are all oracle: You are the living stock and root of truth and wisdom!"

Lord Dalyell was saying without sarcasm that the Earl of Huntley had spoken truth.

Lady Katherine said, "My worthiest lord and father, the kindness of your sweet composition — your personal qualities and the words you just spoke — thus commands the lowest of obedience."

She curtsied to him, and then continued, "You have granted me a liberty so large that I lack skill to choose without the direction of precedent. From precedent I daily learn that by how much more you take off from the roughness of a father, by so much more I am engaged to tender the duty of a daughter."

She meant that the gentler he was as a father, the more dutiful she believed she ought to be as a daughter.

Lady Katherine continued, "As for consideration of birth, degrees of title, and advancement, I neither admire nor slight them. All my efforts shall always aim only at achieving this perfection: To live and die in such a way that you may not blush in any course of mine to acknowledge me as yours."

She wanted her father to never be ashamed of her, and she wanted to act in such a way that he would feel no need to be ashamed of her.

"Kate, Kate, thou grow upon my heart like peace, creating every other hour a jubilee of rejoicing," her father, the Earl of Huntley, replied.

She then said, "To you, my lord of Dalyell, I address some few remaining words. The general public opinion that affirms your merit, even in common tongues proclaims it to be clear and without stain, but in the best tongues, it is proclaimed to be an example that ought to be followed."

"Good wench, good girl, in faith!" the Earl of Huntley said.

He used the word "wench" affectionately.

"As for my part, trust me, I value my own worth at a higher rate because you are pleased to prize it," Lady Katherine said to Lord Dalyell. "If the stream of your professed and solemnly affirmed service — as you term it — runs in a constancy more than a mere compliment, it shall be my delight that your worthy love will lead you to perform worthy actions, and these will powerfully guide you to metaphorically wed a name of honor so every virtuous praise in after-ages shall be your heir, and I in the records of your brave deeds shall be chronicled the spiritual mother of that issue, that glorious issue."

"Issue" is literally a child or children.

Lady Katherine was saying metaphorically that she hoped to be mentioned as the motivation for Lord Dalyell's future performance of splendid deeds.

"Oh, I wish that I were young again!" the Earl of Huntley said. "She'd make me court proud danger, and suck spirit from the famous and honorable reputation I would get by serving her."

Lady Katherine said, "To the present proposal here's all that I dare answer: When I have a ripeness of more experience and some experience of time and I resolve to bargain away the freedom of my youth upon the exchange of wedding vows, I shall desire no surer promise of a match with virtue than such as lives in you."

In other words, when she is more mature and more experienced and decides to marry, she will want to marry someone with Lord Dalyell's virtues and good qualities.

This was a gentle and complimentary way of saying no to Lord Dalyell's proposal of marriage at this time.

"In the meantime my hopes are securely preserved in having you as a friend," Lady Katherine said.

"You are a blessed lady, and you instruct ambition not to soar a farther flight than in the perfumed air of your soft voice," Lord Dalyell replied.

He then said, "My noble Lord of Huntley, you have lent a full extent of generosity to this conversation you have allowed me to have with your daughter, and in return for it you shall command me, your humblest servant."

"Enough," the Earl of Huntley said. "We are still friends, and we will continue to have a hearty love for each other."

He then said, "Oh, Kate, thou are my own!"

The Earl of Crawford, bearing a message from the King, entered the room.

Seeing him approaching, the Earl of Huntley said, "Let's say no more."

He then greeted the King's messenger, "My Lord of Crawford."

"From the King I come, my Lord of Huntley, who in council requires your immediate aid," the Earl of Crawford said.

"Some weighty business?" the Earl of Huntley asked.

"A secretary from a Duke of York, the second son to the late English King Edward IV, concealed — I don't know where — these fourteen years, craves a meeting with our master, and it is said that the Duke — Perkin Warbeck — himself is following the secretary and coming to the court."

The Earl of Crawford's "I don't know where" subtly made the point that he was skeptical that Perkin Warbeck was the real Duke of York.

In fact, Perkin Warbeck was pretending to be one of the deceased sons of the late King Edward IV of England.

"Duke upon Duke," the Earl of Huntley said. "It is well, it is well. Here's contending for majesty."

He could guess that Perkin Warbeck was seeking from King James IV of Scotland help that would install him — Perkin Warbeck — on the throne of England.

The Earl of Huntley's "Duke upon Duke" subtly made the point that he was skeptical that Perkin Warbeck was the real Duke of York.

The Earl of Huntley said to the Earl of Crawford, "My lord, I will go along with you."

The Earl of Crawford said to Lady Katherine, "My service, noble lady!"

Lady Katherine said to Lord Dalyell, "Does it please you to walk, sir?"

Lord Dalyell thought, *Times have their changes; sorrow makes men wise. The sun itself must set as well as rise. So then, why not I?*

He replied out loud, "Fair madam, I wait on you."

— 1.3 —

The Bishop of Durham, Sir Robert Clifford, and Christopher Urswick talked together in an apartment in the Tower of London. The apartment was lit with torches.

Sir Robert Clifford had supported Perkin Warbeck, but he turned against him and was now about to reveal to King Henry VII details of the plot to make Perkin Warbeck King of England. The interrogation was taking place in the Tower of London, where King Henry VII had temporarily moved his court, in part because if Sir Robert Clifford named some high-ranking nobles in the court as traitors, they could be arrested quickly.

The Bishop of Durham said, "You see, Sir Robert Clifford, how confidently King Henry VII, our great master, commits his personal safety to your loyalty; you taste his bounty and his mercy even in this: that at a time of night so late, a place so private as his own chamber, he is pleased to admit you to his favor. Do not falter in your disclosure of the conspiracy; but as you covet a liberal grace and pardon for your follies, so labor to deserve it by revealing all the plots and all the persons who contrive against it."

Christopher Urswick said to Sir Robert Clifford, "Don't remember the witchcraft or the magic, the charms and incantations, which the sorceress of Burgundy — Margaret of Burgundy — cast upon your reason. Sir Robert, be your own friend now and do what is best for you: Tell all you know and free your conscience from guilt. All who respect you stand as guarantees for your honesty and truth. Take care that you do not dally with the King: He is as wise as he is gentle."

"I am miserable, if King Henry VII will not be merciful," Sir Robert Clifford replied.

"The King is coming," Christopher Urswick said.

King Henry VII entered the apartment and said, "Clifford!"

Sir Robert Clifford knelt and said, "Let my weak knees root on the earth, if I appear as leprous in my treacheries before your royal eyes, as to my own eyes I seem to be a monster as a result of my breach of truth."

He had sworn to be loyal to King Henry VII, but he had broken his oath by plotting to help make Perkin Warbeck King.

"Clifford, stand up," King Henry VII said. "For evidence of thy safety, I offer thee my hand."

"It is a sovereign balm for my bruised soul," Sir Robert Clifford said. "I kiss it with greediness."

He kissed the King's hand, rose, and said, "Sir, you're a just master, but I —"

Wanting to get down to business quickly, King Henry VII interrupted, "Tell me, is every detail thou has set down with thine own hand within this paper true? Is it accurate information of all the progress of our enemies' intentions without corruption by anything that is not true?"

"It is as true as I wish Heaven or as I wish my infected honor to be white and morally pure again," Sir Robert Clifford replied.

"We know all, Clifford, fully, since this comet, this airy and insubstantial apparition first discradled himself and moved from Tournai in Belgium into Portugal, and thence advanced his fiery blaze for adoration to the superstitious Irish," King Henry VII said. "Thereupon the tail of this wild comet, conjured into France, sparkled in grotesque flames in the court of King Charles VIII of France. But it shrunk again from there, and, hidden in darkness, stole into Flanders and then landed in England, flourishing the rag — his so-called standard — of counterfeit power on the shore of Kent, from where he was beaten back with shame and scorn, contempt, and slaughter of some naked outlaws."

In July of 1495, Perkin Warbeck sailed to Deal, Kent, with a small force of men, but the citizens of Deal fought and defeated his men. He then sailed to Ireland, as Sir Robert Clifford will inform King Henry VII. For 11 days, he unsuccessfully besieged the Irish port of Waterford, resisted by its citizens. Perkin Warbeck then sailed for Scotland, and in November of 1495, King James IV of Scotland received him.

King Henry VII added, "But tell me what new course now shapes 'Duke' Perkin?"

His use of "Duke" when referring to Perkin Warbeck was sarcastic.

Sir Robert Clifford said, "His new course is for Ireland, mighty Henry; he was so instructed by Stephen Frion, who was formerly a secretary in the French tongue to your sacred excellence, but who is Perkin's tutor now."

"He is a crafty villain, that Frion, Frion," King Henry VII said.

He then said, "You, my Lord of Durham, knew the man well."

The Bishop of Durham said, "He is French both in his heart and in his actions."

This was not a compliment.

King Henry VII said to Sir Robert Clifford, "Some Irish heads work in this mine of treason and support Perkin Warbeck. Name them."

Sir Robert Clifford replied, "They are not any of the best; your good fortune has dulled their spirits. Never has a fraud had such a confused rabble of lost bankrupts for counselors. First is Heron, a bankrupt dealer in textile fabrics. Then are John a-Water, who is sometimes Mayor of Cork, Ireland, and a tailor named Skelton and a legal clerk called Astley. Whatever these wish to speak about, Perkin must listen to; but Frion, who is more cunning and intelligent than these dull capacities, still prompts Perkin to fly to Scotland to young King James IV and appeal to him for aid. This is the most recent of all their resolutions."

"Still more Frion!" King Henry VII said. "Pestilent adder, he will hiss out poison that is as dangerous as it is infectious. We must equal him in cunning.

"Clifford, thou have spoken well and to the heart of the matter and given us good information; we give thee life. But, Clifford, there are unknown conspirators of our own people who remain behind in England; who are they, Clifford? Name those conspirators who are in England, and we are friends, and then we will rest. This is thy last task."

"Oh, sir, here I must break a most unlawful oath to keep a just one," Sir Robert Clifford said.

The very unlawful oath was the oath of allegiance he had made to the conspirators; the just oath was the oath of allegiance he had made to King Henry VII.

"Well, well, be brief, be brief," King Henry VII said.

Naming the conspirators who supported Perkin Warbeck, Sir Robert Clifford said, "The first in rank shall be John Ratcliffe, Lord Fitzwater. Then are Sir Simon Mountford and Sir Thomas Thwaites, with William Dawbeney, Chessoner, Astwood, Worseley the Dean of St. Paul's Cathredral, two other friars, and Robert Ratcliffe."

"Churchmen are turned devils," King Henry VII said, and then he asked, "These are the principal conspirators?"

"One more remains unnamed, whom I could willingly forget," Sir Robert Clifford said.

"Ha, Clifford!" King Henry VII said. "One more?"

"Great sir, do not hear him," Sir Robert Clifford said.

He meant 1) Do not hear his name, or 2) Do not listen to what he will want to tell you.

Sir Robert Clifford continued, "For when Sir William Stanley, your Lord Chamberlain, shall come into the list, as he is chief, I shall lose credit with you — yet this lord who is the last named is the first conspirator against you."

"Urswick, bring the torch!" King Henry VII said.

He brought the torch.

King Henry VII then said, "View well my face, sirs; is there any blood left in it?"

"You alter strangely, sir," the Bishop of Durham said.

"Alter, Lord Bishop!" King Henry VII said. "Why, Clifford stabbed me, or I dreamed he stabbed me."

He said to Sir Robert Clifford, "Sirrah, it is a custom with the guilty to think that they remove their own moral stains by laying aspersions on some people nobler than themselves. Lies accompany and serve treasons, as I find it here. Thy life again is forfeit; I recall and take back my word of mercy, for I know thou dare to repeat the name no more."

"I dare, and once more, upon my knowledge, name Sir William Stanley both in his counsel and his financial support the chief assistant to the feigned Duke of York," Sir Robert Clifford replied.

"Most strange!" the Bishop of Durham said.

"Most wicked!" Christopher Urswick said

"Yet again, tell me once more," King Henry VII said to Sir Robert Clifford.

"Sir William Stanley is your secret enemy, and, when the time is fit, he will openly profess it," Sir Robert Clifford replied.

"Sir William Stanley! Who? Sir William Stanley! My Lord Chamberlain, my counselor, the love and the pleasure of my court, my bosom friend, the charge and the control of access to me and the provider of my own personal security, the keys and secrets of my treasury, the all of all I am!" King Henry VII said. "I am unhappy. Misery of confidence, let me turn traitor to my own person and yield my scepter up to Edward's sister and her bastard Duke!"

Edward's sister and her bastard Duke were Margaret of Burgundy and Perkin Warbeck.

"You lose your steadiness of temper," the Bishop of Durham said.

"Sir William Stanley!" King Henry VII said. "Oh, do not blame me; he, it was only he, who, having rescued me in the Battle of Bosworth Field from Richard's bloody sword, snatched from his head the Kingly crown, and placed it first on my head."

At the Battle of Bosworth Field in 1485, Sir William Stanley, who had supported King Richard III, a Yorkist, brought in his soldiers at the last moment to support Henry Tudor, who won the battle and became King Henry VII, the first Tudor King.

"He never failed me," King Henry VII said. "In what way have I deserved to lose this good man's heart, or he his own?"

"The night wastes away," Christopher Urswick said. "This passion ill becomes you. Prepare against your danger."

"Let it be so," King Henry VII said. "Urswick, command Stanley to go immediately to his chamber — it is well we are in the Tower of London — and set a guard on him."

King Henry VII had moved himself and his court to the Tower of London in order to question Sir Robert Clifford.

He continued, "Clifford, go to bed. You must lodge here tonight. We'll talk with you tomorrow."

He then said to all present, "My sad soul divines strange troubles."

Lord Giles Dawbeney called from outside the apartment, "Ho! The King! The King! I must have entrance to the King."

"That is Dawbeney's voice," King Henry VII said. "Admit him. What new tumultuous conflagrations pile up now and keep our eyes from rest?"

Lord Giles Dawbeney entered the apartment.

"What is the news?" King Henry VII asked Lord Giles Dawbeney.

"Ten thousand Cornishmen, begrudging to pay your taxes for war against Scotland, have gathered together an army. Led by a blacksmith and a lawyer, they make their way for London, and to them is joined Lord Audley. As they march, their number daily increases; they are —"

Michael Joseph, a blacksmith; Thomas Flammock, a lawyer; and Lord Audley were the leaders of the Cornish rebellion.

King Henry VII finished Lord Giles Dawbeney's sentence, "— rascals! Talk no more. Such rascals are not worthy of my thoughts tonight. Let's all go to bed, and if I cannot sleep, I'll stay awake.

"When counsels fail, and there's in man no trust, even then an arm from Heaven fights for the just."

CHAPTER 2

The Countess of Crawford, Lady Katherine, Jane Douglas, and some other ladies were gathered in a balcony overlooking King James IV of Scotland's presence chamber in his palace in Edinburgh.

The Countess of Crawford's husband was the Earl of Crawford, the man who had summoned the Earl of Huntley to the King's presence.

The Earl of Huntley and the Earl of Crawford had seemed skeptical that Perkin Warbeck was the real Duke of York. These ladies' conversation would make it clear that they were also skeptical.

The Countess of Crawford said, "Come, ladies, here's a solemn preparation for the reception of this English prince. Our King of Scotland intends to show him more than ordinary grace. It would be a pity now if the English prince should prove to be a counterfeit."

"Bless the young man," Lady Katherine said. "If he should prove to be a counterfeit, our nation would be laughed at throughout Christendom for being innocent, naive souls! My father has a weak stomach — a disinclination — for the business, madam, were it not that the King must not be crossed and thwarted."

Lady Katherine's father, the Earl of Huntley, wanted no part of Perkin Warbeck.

The Countess of Crawford now ironically praised Perkin Warbeck's followers for hiding their identities as princes under the cover of being members of the working class.

She said, "The English prince, Perkin Warbeck, brings a goodly troop, they say, of gallants with him. But they are very modest people, for they strive not to spread abroad their names too much; their godfathers may be beholden to them, but their fathers scarcely owe them thanks."

She, being cynical, meant this: While in "hiding," Perkin Warbeck's followers had taken names different from the names of their fathers, pleasing their godfathers because they could deny being associated with them but displeasing their fathers because they had denied their fathers' names.

The Countess of Crawford added, "They are disguised princes, brought up, it seems, to work in honest trades, but it doesn't matter: They will break forth in season."

She meant that they would reveal their "true" princely natures at the right time. Or she meant that their true identities as non-princes would be revealed at the right time.

Jane Douglas said, "If they do not break forth, they will break out, for most of them are broken — bankrupt — according to reports."

She may have meant that they would break out in rebellion. Being bankrupt, they had much to gain and little to lose. Or she may have meant that, being bankrupt, they would break out of debtors' prison.

A flourish of trumpets sounded.

Jane Douglas said, "The King is arriving."

"Let us observe them and be silent," Lady Katherine said.

King James IV of Scotland, the Earl of Huntley, the Earl of Crawford, Lord Dalyell, and other noblemen entered the presence chamber.

King James IV said, "The right of Kings, my lords, extends not only to the safe conservation of their own crowns and subjects, but also to the aid of such allied sovereigns as change of time and state has often hurled down from full-of-care crowns to undergo an exercise of endurance in both kinds of fortunes: good and bad.

"So the English King Richard I, surnamed Coeur-de-Lion, and so Robert Bruce, our royal ancestor, forced by the trial of the wrongs they felt, both sought and found supplies and reinforcements from foreign Kings to help repossess what was their own."

Richard I the Lionheart (1157-1199) reigned as King of England from 1189 to 1199. In the 1180s, King Richard I sought help from King Philip II (known also as Philip Augustus) of France in defending the Duchy of Aquitaine, which Richard had ruled since 1172.

Robert the Bruce (1274-1329) reigned as King of Scotland from 1306 to 1329. In 1295 King Robert I sought and received refuge from King Edward I of England.

King James IV continued, "Then don't grudge, lords, to help a much distressed prince: Perkin Warbeck.

"King Charles VIII of France and Maximilian of Bohemia both have ratified his credit and authenticity by their letters. Shall we, then, be distrustful? No. Compassion is one rich jewel that shines in our crown, and we will continue to have it shine there."

"Do as you will, sir," the Earl of Huntley said.

"The young Duke is at hand," King James IV said. "Dalyell, from us first greet him, and conduct him here. Then the Earl of Crawford shall meet him next, and the Earl of Huntley shall meet him last of all.

"Present him to our arms."

Lord Dalyell exited to carry out his orders.

King James IV ordered, "Let sprightly music sound while majesty encounters majesty."

Music played.

Lord Dalyell returned with Perkin Warbeck, followed at a distance by Frion, Heron, Skelton, Astley, and John a-Water.

The Earl of Crawford advanced and received Perkin Warbeck at the door, and then the Earl of Huntley saluted Perkin Warbeck and presented him to King James IV. The Scottish King and Perkin Warbeck embraced. The Scottish noblemen slightly saluted Perkin Warbeck's followers.

Perkin Warbeck said, "Most high, most mighty King! That now there stands before your eyes, in presence of your peers, a subject — myself — of the rarest kind of pity that has in any age touched noble hearts, the widely known story of a prince's ruin has made too apparent. Europe knows, and all the western world knows, what persecution has raged in malice against us" — he was using the royal plural — "the sole heir to the great throne of the old Plantagenets."

The first Plantagenet King was King Henry II (1154-1189). From 1154 until 1485, when King Richard III died, all English Kings were Plantagenets. The Lancaster family and the York family were Plantagenets.

King Henry VII was the first Tudor King. His father was Edmund Tudor, and so King Henry VII was a member of the House of Tudor. However, through the female line he could trace his ancestry back to King Edward III of the House of Plantagenet. His mother was Lady Margaret Beaufort, a great-granddaughter of John of Gaunt, Duke of Lancaster, who was the fourth son of King Edward III.

If Perkin Warbeck's claim to be the Duke of York, King Edward IV's son, had been true, he would have a stronger claim to the throne of England than King Henry VII. Perkin Warbeck, however, was wrong when he claimed to be "the sole heir to the great throne of the old Plantagenets." One son of the Earl of Clarence, brother to King Edward IV and King Richard III, still lived: the Earl of Warwick.

Perkin Warbeck introduced his story, in which he would explain why he — the "Duke of York" — was still alive and where he had been for the past fourteen years:

"How from our nursery we have been hurried to the sanctuary, from the sanctuary forced to the prison, from the prison dragged by cruel hands to the tormentor's fury, is registered already in the book of all men's tongues, whose true telling draws compassion, melted into weeping eyes and bleeding souls, but our misfortunes since have ranged a larger journey through foreign lands, protected in our innocence by Heaven."

Perkin Warbeck first explained why he was still alive. This was necessary since most people thought that King Edward V and the Duke of York (whom Perkin Warbeck was pretending to be) had been murdered in the Tower of London by the order of the future King Richard III:

"King Edward V, our brother, in his tragedy quenched his murderers' hot thirst of blood, whose contract to commit murder paid them their wages of despair and horror. The softness of my childhood smiled upon the roughness of their task, and robbed them farther of hearts to dare or hands to execute. Great King, they spared my life; the butchers spared it. They reported to the tyrant, my unnatural and inhuman uncle, King Richard III, an oath concerning my 'death.'"

He meant that the murderers told King Richard III a partial truth — they had killed the young King Edward V — but then they had lied and said that they had also killed the young Duke of York. However, the real truth (as far as historians know) is that murderers killed both boys, probably in 1483, when they disappeared. King Edward V was then twelve years old, and the Duke of York was nine years old.

Perkin Warbeck next explained where he had been raised after his life was "spared":

"I was conveyed with secrecy and speed to Tournai, where I was fostered by a common family, and taught to forget myself and not reveal my true identity."

Perkin Warbeck finally explained why he had chosen to reveal his "true" identity recently:

"But as I grew in years, I grew in sense both of fear and of disdain. I was in fear of the tyrant Richard III whose power swayed the throne then: I was afraid that he would again attempt to kill me.

"But when disdain of living so unknown, in such a servile and abject lowness, prompted me to thoughts of recollecting who I was, I shook off my bondage, and made haste to let my aunt of Burgundy acknowledge me as her kinsman, heir to England's crown, which was snatched by Henry from Richard III's head — a thing scarcely known in the world."

Perkin Warbeck declined to refer to King Henry VII as King, preferring to call him simply "Henry."

King James IV said, "My lord, it is not consistent with your counsel and purpose now to fly upon and use invective. If you can provide convincing evidence of what you have discoursed in every circumstance, we will not delay by meditating on our answer, but instead be ready to help you in your cause."

Perkin Warbeck replied, "You are a wise and just King, by the powers above reserved and set apart, beyond all other aids, to plant me in my own inheritance, to marry these two kingdoms as allies in a love never to be divorced while time is time.

"As for the manner, first of my escape, of my transportation elsewhere next, of my life since then, the means and persons who were instruments of my escape, great sir, it is fit I pass all this over in silence, reserving the relation to the secrecy of your own princely ear, since it concerns some great ones yet living, and others dead, whose descendants might be questioned. In return for your bounty, your royal munificence to him who seeks it, we vow hereafter to conduct ourself as if we were your own and natural brother, omitting no occasion in our person to express a gratitude beyond precedent."

King James IV said, "He who can utter the language of a King must be more than just a subject, and such language is thine. Take this for your answer: Be whatever thou are, thou never shall repent that thou have put thy cause and person into my protection. Cousin of York, thus once more we embrace thee. Welcome to James of Scotland!"

Kings called other Kings "cousin." This did not necessarily imply a biological relationship.

King James IV continued, "As for thy safety, know that such people as do not love thee shall never wrong thee.

"Come, we will taste a while our court-delights, pleasantly daydream away past afflictions, and then proceed to high adventures of honor on the battlefield.

"On, lead on!

"Both thou and thine are ours, and we will guard all of you.

"Lead on!"

Everyone exited except the ladies on the balcony.

The Countess of Crawford said, "I have not seen a gentleman of braver appearance or better carriage. His bad fortune in life so far does not dismay him."

She then said to Lady Katherine, "Madam, you're very emotional."

"Beshrew me, but his words have touched me deeply, as if his cause concerned me," Lady Katherine said. "I would pity him if he would prove to be someone other than he seems to be."

She meant that she would pity Perkin Warbeck if he turned out to be a fraud.

The Earl of Crawford returned and said, "Ladies, the King commands your presence immediately for the reception of the Duke of York."

"The Duke of York must then be entertained and the King obeyed," Lady Katherine said. "It is our duty."

"We will all attend on him," the Countess of Crawford said.

All went to the reception for Perkin Warbeck.

— 2.2 —

King Henry VII, the Earl of Oxford, the Earl of Surrey, and the Bishop of Durham met in the Tower of London. They talked about Sir William Stanley — the Lord Chamberlain — who had been convicted of treason in a trial by his peers.

"Have you convicted my Lord Chamberlain?" King Henry VII asked.

"His treasons convicted him, sir," the Bishop of Durham replied. "They were as clear and manifest as they were foul and dangerous; besides, the guilt of his conspiracy pressed and oppressed him so nearly and closely that it drew from him a freely made confession without persistent requests."

"Oh, Lord Bishop, his willing confession argued shame and sorrow for his folly, and it must not stand in evidence against our mercy and the softness of our nature," King Henry VII said. "The rigor and extremity of law is sometimes too, too bitter, but we carry a chancery court of equity, appeal, and pity in our bosom. I hope we may reprieve him from the sentence of death — I hope we may."

"You may, you may," the Bishop of Durham said, "and in so doing you may persuade your subjects that the title of York is better, and indeed more just and lawful, than your title of Lancaster! That is what Stanley believes. If that belief is not treason in the highest degree, then we are all traitors, and we are all perjured and false, all of us who have taken an oath to Henry and the justice of Henry's title. Oxford, Surrey, Dawbeney, and all your other peers of state and church are forsworn and perjured, and Stanley alone is true to Heaven and England's lawful heir!"

The Bishop of Durham was sarcastic: If King Henry VII were to fail to sentence Lord Stanley to death, then it would be evidence that Lord Stanley was right to support Perkin Warbeck's claim to the throne of England and all the nobles who had sworn oaths of loyalty to Henry VII were wrong to have done so.

"By Vere's old honors, I'll cut the throat of anyone who dares to speak such treason," the Earl of Oxford said.

"Vere" was the Earl of Oxford's family name: The Earl of Oxford was referring to the honors of his family.

"It is a quarrel to engage a soul in," the Earl of Surrey said.

"What a turmoil is here to keep my gratitude unadulterated and perfect!" King Henry VII said. "Stanley was once my friend, and he came in time to save my life at the Battle of Bosworth Field; yet, to say the truth, my lords, the man delayed his help long enough to endanger my life.

"But I could see no more into his heart than what his outward actions presented. And for his outward actions I have rewarded him so fully that there lacked nothing in our gift to reward his merit, so I thought, unless I should divide my crown with him, and give him half, although now I well perceive it would hardly have served his turn and satisfied him without the whole crown.

"But I am charitable, lords; let justice continue on in execution — both operation and capital punishment — while I mourn the loss of one whom I esteemed a friend."

"Sir, he is coming this way," the Bishop of Durham said.

"If he speaks to me, I could deny him nothing," King Henry VII said. "To prevent it, I must withdraw. Please, lords, give him my best wishes for his last peace, which I will pray for, as will he. That done, it concerns us to consult about other following troubles."

King Henry VII exited.

"I am glad he's gone," the Earl of Oxford said. "I swear upon my life that he would have pardoned the traitor, had he seen him."

"He is a King composed of gentleness," the Earl of Surrey said.

"Which is rare and unheard of," the Bishop of Durham said. "But it is true that every man is nearest to himself and looks out for himself, and the King observes that truth, as is fitting that he should."

Sir William Stanley, Christopher Urswick, and Lord Giles Dawbeney entered the scene. The executioner and the confessor accompanied them.

"May I speak with Clifford — the man who accused me of treason — before I shake off this piece of frailty that is my body?" Sir William Stanley asked.

"You shall," Lord Giles Dawbeney replied. "He has been sent for."

"I must not see the King?" Sir William Stanley asked.

"These lords and I have been sent to you from him," the Bishop of Durham replied. "He bade us say that he commends his compassion to your thoughts. He wishes that the laws of England could remit the forfeit of your life as willingly as he would in the sweetness of his nature forget your trespass, but however your body fall into dust, he vows — the King himself vows — to keep a requiem for your soul, as for a friend closely treasured in his bosom."

"Without remembrance of your errors past, I come to take my leave, and wish you Heaven," the Earl of Oxford said.

"And I do, too," the Earl of Surrey said. "May good angels guard you!"

"Oh, the King, next to my soul, shall be the most immediate subject of my last prayers," Sir William Stanley said. "My grave Lord of Durham, and my Lords of Oxford, Surrey, Giles Dawbeney, and all, accept from a poor dying man a farewell. I was once as you are now — I was great and stood hopeful of many flourishing years, but fate and time have wheeled about and revolved, to turn me into nothing."

William Stanley had been high and fortunate on the Wheel of Fortune, but it had turned, and he was now low and unfortunate and about to die.

"Sir Robert Clifford comes — the man, Sir William, you so desire to speak with," Lord Giles Dawbeney said.

"Closely observe their meeting," the Bishop of Durham said quietly. The soon-to-be-beheaded Sir William Stanley was about to meet the man who had accused him of treason.

Sir Robert Clifford entered the scene and said, "Sir William Stanley, I am glad that your conscience before your end has with your confession so emptied every burden that weighed it down that you can clearly witness how far I have proceeded in a duty that concerned both my truth and the state's safety."

"Mercy, how dear is life to such as hug it!" Sir William Stanley said. "Come here; by this token think about me!"

He licked his finger and then made a cross on Clifford's face with it.

"This token!" Sir Robert Clifford said. "What! I am abused and wronged!"

"You are not," Sir William Stanley said. "I wet upon your cheeks a holy sign — the cross, which is the Christian's badge and the traitor's infamy."

The cross is the symbol of Christianity, and crucifixion was the Roman penalty for treason.

"Wear, Clifford, to thy grave this painted emblem," Sir William Stanley said. "Water shall never wash it off; all eyes that gaze upon thy face shall read there written a state-informer's character — a sign that is uglier when stamped on a noble name than when stamped on a base name. May the heavens forgive thee!

"Please, my lords, let there be no exchange of words; this man and I have used too many."

"Shall I be disgraced without making a reply?" Sir Robert Clifford said.

"Give losers such as Sir William Stanley permission to talk," the Bishop of Durham said. "His soon-to-be loss of life is irrecoverable."

"Once more, to all a long farewell!" Sir William Stanley said. "May the best of greatness — God — preserve the King! My next suit is, my lords, to be remembered to my noble brother, Derby, my much-grieved brother."

Sir Thomas Stanley, first Earl of Derby, was Sir William Stanley's older brother. He was also King Henry VII's stepfather.

Sir William Stanley continued, "Oh, persuade him that I shall be no permanent blemish to his house in chronicles written in another age."

He expected that future histories would treat his memory well.

He continued, "My heart bleeds for him and for his sighs: Tell him that he must not think the name and title of Derby, nor being husband to King Henry VII's mother, the league with peers, and the smiles of Lady Fortune can secure his peace above the state of man."

The natural state of man was one in which one could be high on the Wheel of Fortune and then be low on the Wheel of Fortune. The natural state of man was one of uncertainty.

Sir William Stanley continued, "I take my leave to travel to my dust. Subjects deserve their deaths whose Kings are just."

He did not say that King Henry VII was just.

He continued, "Come, confessor.

"Onward with thy axe, friendly executioner, onward!"

He was led off to be beheaded.

"Was I called here by a traitor's breath to be upbraided?" Sir Robert Clifford said. "Lords, the King shall know it."

King Henry VII reentered, carrying a white staff that had been Lord William Stanley's staff of office as Lord Chamberlain.

He said, "The King does know it, sir; the King has heard what he or you could say. We have given credit to every point of Clifford's information, the only evidence against Stanley's head. He dies for it."

He then asked, sarcastically, "Are you pleased?"

"Am I pleased, my lord!" Sir Robert Clifford said.

"No echoes," King Henry VII said. "As for your service, we dismiss you from further attendance on the court; take your ease, and live at home; but as you love your life, don't stir away from London without first getting permission from us. We'll think about your reward for the information you have provided us. Leave!"

"I go, sir," Sir Robert Clifford said.

He exited.

King Henry VII said, "May all our griefs die with Stanley!

"Take this staff of office, Giles Dawbeney; henceforth, you shall be our Lord Chamberlain."

"I am your humble servant," Lord Chamberlain Giles Dawbeney replied.

"We are followed by enemies at home, who will not cease to seek their own ruin," King Henry VII said. "It is most true that the Cornish under Audley have marched on as far as Winchester — but let them come. Our forces are in readiness; we'll catch them in their own snares."

Winchester is within sixty miles of London.

Lord Chamberlain Giles Dawbeney said, "Your army, being mustered, consists in all, of horsemen and footmen, in number at least twenty-six thousand. These are men who are daring and able, resolute to fight, and loyal in their vows to you."

"We know it, Giles Dawbeney," King Henry VII said. "For them we give these orders.

"Oxford in chief, assisted by bold Essex and the Earl of Suffolk, shall lead on the first division.

"That will be your charge."

The Earl of Oxford replied, "I humbly thank your majesty."

King Henry VII continued, "The next military division we assign to Giles Dawbeney. These must be men of action, for on those the fortune of our fortunes must rely.

"The last and main division ourself commands in person. It is as ready to turn the tide of battle at all times as it is to consummate an assured victory."

"The King is as always oracular," Lord Chamberlain Giles Dawbeney said.

In other words, King Henry VII always told the truth just as if he were an oracle, according to Lord Chamberlain Giles Dawbeney.

"But, Surrey, we have employment of more toil for thee," King Henry VII said. "For our intelligence comes swiftly to us that James IV of Scotland recently has welcomed Perkin the counterfeit with more than common grace and respect, indeed, he courts him with rare favors. The Scot is young and forward; we must look for a sudden storm coming to England from the north, from Scotland.

"In order to withstand the Scots, the Bishop of Durham shall go posthaste to Norham to fortify the border castle there and secure the frontiers against an invasion.

"The Earl of Surrey shall follow soon, with such an army as may relieve the bishop, and encounter at every opportunity the death-daring Scots. You all know your responsibilities; it is now a time to execute, not talk. Heaven is our guard still. War must breed peace; such is the fate of Kings.

— 2.3 —

The Earl of Crawford and Lord Dalyell talked together in an apartment in the palace at Edinburgh. Neither man believed that Perkin Warbeck was the Duke of York.

"It is more than strange," the Earl of Crawford said. "My reason cannot answer such an argument made from fine imposture, expressed in such a witchcraft of persuasion that it fashions impossibilities as if appearance could deceive truth itself."

He was saying that he could not rationally believe that Perkin Warbeck had succeeded in making King James IV believe that he, Perkin Warbeck, was the Duke of York and the rightful heir to the English throne.

He added, "This dukeling mushroom has doubtless charmed and put a spell on the King."

The word "mushroom" was used to describe someone who came out of nowhere to achieve high status. The word was appropriate because mushrooms grow overnight.

According to the Earl of Crawford, the best explanation for King James IV's belief in Perkin Warbeck was that Perkin Warbeck had put a magic spell on him.

Lord Dalyell said, "He courts the ladies as if his strength of language chained attention by power of prerogative — by the privilege of royalty."

"It maddened my very soul to hear our master King James IV's proposal," the Earl of Crawford said.

King James IV wanted to marry a high-ranking Scottish woman to Perkin Warbeck. This was a way of ensuring loyalty between two Kings and peace between two countries.

The Earl of Crawford continued, "What guarantee both of friendship and honor must of necessity ensue upon a match between some noble of our nation and this 'brave prince,' indeed!"

"It will prove too fatal," Lord Dalyell said. "Wise Huntley fears the threatening. May God bless and protect the lady from such a ruin!"

Events would show that the lady being mentioned as a wife for Perkin Warbeck was Lady Katherine, the Earl of Huntley's daughter.

The Earl of Crawford said, "How the 'Privy Council' of this young Phaëthon screw their faces into a gravity their trades, good people, were never guilty of! The meanest of them dreams of at least an office in the state."

Phaëthon went to his father, the god Apollo, and asked to be allowed to drive the Sun-chariot across the sky and bring light to the world. But Phaëthon, doomed youth, was unable to control the stallions, and they ran wildly away with the Sun-chariot, wreaking havoc and destruction upon Humankind and the world by making the chariot come so close to the Earth that it set the Earth on fire. The King of the gods, Jupiter, saved Humankind and the world by throwing a thunderbolt at Phaëthon and killing him.

By calling Perkin Warbeck "Phaëthon," the Earl of Crawford was saying the he had suddenly risen high but that the rise would end with a sudden fall.

The use of "Privy Council" to refer to Perkin Warbeck's followers was also ironic. The members of the Privy Council were a King's closest and most trusted advisors. To the Earl of Crawford, Perkin Warbeck's followers were greedy, ambitious common people.

"Surely, they don't seek the hangman's office," Lord Dalyell said. "That office is already spoken for — the executioner will do service to their rogueships."

Lord Dalyell agreed with the Earl of Crawford that Perkin Warbeck's followers were greedy, ambitious lowlifes, and so he used "rogueships" rather than "lordships" to refer to them.

Seeing King James IV and the Earl of Huntley coming, Lord Dalyell said, "Silence!"

King James IV and the Earl of Huntley arrived. The Earl of Huntley had been trying to convince the King that Perkin Warbeck was a fraud. The Earl of Huntley certainly did not want his daughter — Lady Katherine — to marry a fraud.

"Do not argue against our will," King James IV said, using the royal plural. "We have descended somewhat — as we may term it — too familiarly and unceremoniously from the justice of our birthright, to examine the strength of your allegiance — sir, we have — but we find the strength of your allegiance short of duty."

"Break my heart," the Earl of Huntley said. "Do, do, King! Have my services, my loyalty — Heaven knows that they are always untainted — draw upon me contempt now in my old age, when I lacked only a minute before I enjoyed a peace that would not be troubled — my last peace, my long peace that will follow my death! Let me be a dotard, a senile old man, a bedlamite, a madman, a poor sot, or whatever you please to have me, so long as you will not stain your blood, your own blood, royal sir, though mixed with mine, by marriage of this girl — Katherine, my daughter — to a vagabond. Take, take my head, sir — as long as my tongue can wag, it cannot call him — Perkin Warbeck — anything other than a vagabond."

"Kings are counterfeits in your opinion, grave oracle, if they are not here and now set on their thrones with scepters in their fists," King James IV said. "But perpetuate your own loss of reputation; it is our pleasure to give our cousin York our kinswoman the Lady Katherine as his wife. My royal instinct that Perkin Warbeck is truly of royal birth points out the honor that she shall be married to, although you, her peevish father, are attempting to usurp our already-made decision and want to make a different decision regarding her."

"Oh, it is well, exceeding well!" the Earl of Huntley said. "I never was ambitious of using congees — bowing ceremonially — to my daughter-Queen. A Queen? Perhaps a quean!"

A quean is a whore.

The Earl of Huntley said to Lord Dalyell, whom he knew loved Lady Katherine and would not want to hear her called a whore, "Forgive me, Dalyell, thou honorable gentleman."

He then asked, "Does anyone here dare to speak even one word to support what I am saying?"

"Cruel misery!" Lord Dalyell said.

"The lady, gracious prince, maybe has settled her affection on some former choice," the Earl of Crawford said. "She may love someone other than Perkin Warbeck."

"Forcing her to marry someone would prove to be tyranny," Lord Dalyell said.

"I thank you heartily for speaking up," the Earl of Huntley said. "Let any yeoman — any respectable commoner landowner — of our nation demand as a right an interest in the girl. If that should happen, then the King may add a marriage settlement of promotion in titles, worthy a free consent; but now he pulls down what old merit and desert have built."

The Earl of Huntley believed that if a yeoman were to want to marry Lady Katherine, King James IV could make the marriage desirable by giving honorable titles to the yeoman and raising his social status, but by making Lady Katherine marry Perkin Warbeck, he was lowering her because although Perkin Warbeck appeared to be noble, his "nobility" would disappear as soon as he were revealed to be an imposter.

Of course, the Earl of Huntley vastly preferred Lord Dalyell rather than Perkin Warbeck as a husband for his daughter. That could happen if King James IV were to give honorable titles to Lord Dalyell.

"Cease your attempts at persuasion," King James IV said. "I violate no pawns of faith, no pledges of betrothal, and no promises of marriage, and I do not intrude on private loves."

King James IV was unaware that Lord Dalyell loved Lady Katherine.

He continued, "Virtuous Kate's consent can justify my having played the orator for the kingly Duke of York: She can give her consent to handing over her future happiness to a husband of our providing. The Welsh Harry henceforth shall therefore know, and tremble to acknowledge, that the counterfeit idol of his political machinations shall not frighten the lawful owner from a kingdom. We are resolved — we have made up our mind."

The Welsh Harry was King Henry VII, whose family — the Tudors — had Welsh origins. King Henry VII's grandfather, Owen Tudor, was Welsh. King James IV of Scotland, like Perkin Warbeck, declined to call Henry the King of England.

"Some of thy subjects' hearts, King James, will bleed for this," the Earl of Huntley said.

Backing Perkin Warbeck's claim to be King of England meant war against King Henry VII.

"Then their bloods shall be nobly spent," King James IV said.

Using the royal plural, he said, "No more disputes; whoever contradicts us is not our friend."

"Farewell, daughter!" the Earl of Huntley said. "My care by one is lessened — I thank the King for it. I and my griefs will dance now."

Several people entered the scene. Perkin Warbeck led them as he and Lady Katherine held hands and exchanged courteous words. The others were the Countess of Crawford, Jane Douglas, Frion, Astley, John a-Water, Heron, and Skelton.

"Look, lords, look," the Earl of Huntley said. "Here they are, hand in hand already!"

King James IV said to the Earl of Huntley, "Silence, old frenzied man!"

He then said about Perkin Warbeck, "How like a King he looks! Lords, just observe the confidence of his aspect; dross cannot cleave to so pure a metal — royal youth! Plantagenet undoubted!"

When metal is purified, the impurities known as dross are left behind.

The Earl of Huntley said sarcastically to himself, "Ho, splendid! Youth, but no Plantagenet, by our lady the Virgin Mary, yet, whether by the red rose or by the white rose."

In the Wars of the Roses, the emblem of the Yorkists was the white rose, while the emblem of the Lancastrians was the red rose. Margaret of Burgundy was a Yorkist, while King Henry VII was a Lancastrian through the female line. The Earl of Huntley believed that Perkin Warbeck was a fraud and therefore had no rose of either color as an emblem. Both the Yorkists and the Lancastrians were Plantagenets.

Perkin Warbeck said to Lady Katherine, "A union between us settles possession in a monarchy of love — this possession will be established as rightly as is my inheritance of the crown of England. Acknowledge me as sovereign of this kingdom that is your heart, fair princess, and the hand of Providence shall crown you Queen of me and my best fortunes."

"That is where my obedience is a duty, my lord," Lady Katherine replied. "Love owes true service."

"Shall I?" Perkin Warbeck asked the King.

He meant, "Shall I marry her?"

"Cousin, yes," King James IV answered. "Enjoy her; from my hand accept your bride."

King James IV joined their hands together, and then said, "And may all who grieve at such an equal pledge of marriage vows live at enmity with comfort!"

He then said to Lady Katherine, "You are the prince's wife now."

"By your gift, sir," Lady Katherine said.

"Thus I take seizure of my own," Perkin Warbeck said.

"I lack yet a father's blessing," Lady Katherine said. "Let me find it."

She knelt and said, "Humbly upon my knees I seek it."

Her father, the Earl of Huntley, said, "I am Huntley, old Alexander Gordon, a plain subject, neither more nor less; and, lady, if you wish for a blessing, you must bend your knees to Heaven, for Heaven did give you to me.

"Alas, alas — what would you have me say?

"May all the happiness my prayers ever asked to fall upon you preserve you in your virtues!"

Lady Katherine rose.

"Please, Dalyell, come with me," the Earl of Huntley said, "for I feel thy griefs are as great as mine; let's steal away and cry together."

"My hopes are in their ruins," Lord Dalyell said.

The Earl of Huntley and Lord Dalyell exited.

"Good, kind Huntley is overjoyed," King James IV said. "A fitting ceremonial observance shall perfect these delights.

"Crawford, await our order for the preparation of the fitting ceremonial observance."

Everyone exited except Frion, Heron, Skelton, John a-Water, and Astley. These were Perkin Warbeck's followers and advisors.

"Now, worthy gentlemen," Frion said, "haven't I followed my undertakings with success? Here's entrance into a certainty above a hope."

The entrance was into King James IV's court. The certainty was of success, and certainty of success was better than a hope of success.

The other followers' language used the words of the trades they had learned.

John Heron, a dealer in textile fabrics, said, "Hopes are but hopes; I was always confident, when I traded just in remnants of cloth, that my stars had reserved me for the title of a Viscount at least. Honor is honor, whatever materials it is cut out of."

Edward Skelton, a tailor, said, "My brother Heron has very wisely delivered his opinion, for he who threads his needle with the sharp eyes of industry shall in time go like a through-stitch goes through cloth with the new suit of preferment and advancement."

"That was spoken to the purpose, my fine-witted brother Skelton," Nicholas Astley, a legal clerk, said, "for as no indenture, aka contract, but has its counterpane, aka counterpart or copy of a contract, no *noverint*, aka contract, but his condition, aka way of validating a contract, or defeasance, aka way of nullifying a contract, so no right but may have claim, no claim but may have possession, any act of Parliament to the contrary notwithstanding."

The *noverint* (legal bond or contract) got its name from the opening Latin words of the legal document: *noverint universi.* This means, "Let everyone know."

Frion said, "You are all read and learned in mysteries of state, and you are all quick of understanding, deep in judgment, and active in resolution; and it is a pity that such counsel should lie buried in obscurity.

"But why, in such a time and cause of triumph, stands the judicious Mayor of Cork so silent? Believe it, sir, as English Richard prospers, you must not miss out on employment of a high nature."

The "English Richard" Frion mentioned was Perkin Warbeck, who was impersonating Richard, the Duke of York.

John a-Water, a politician, said, "If men may be credited in their mortality — that is, if merely mortal men may be believed — which I dare not peremptorily aver but they may or may not be, presumptions by this marriage are then, truly, of fruitful expectation. Or else I must not justify and uphold other men's belief, more than others should rely on mine."

"Pith of experience!" Frion said. "Those who have borne office weigh every word before it can drop from them. But, noble counselors, since now the present circumstances require in point of honor — please don't misunderstand me — some service to our lord, it is fitting that the Scots should not monopolize all the glory to themselves at this so grand and eminent solemnity — the wedding of Perkin Warbeck and Lady Katherine."

Often, guests would perform a masque, a dramatic presentation often including music and dance, on such occasions.

By saying "please don't misunderstand me," Frion was apologizing for using the word "honor" — the people he was talking to did not deserve the honor of the nobility that they claimed to possess.

Skelton the tailor said, "The Scots! The proposal that they get all the honor is defied. I had rather, for my part, without trial of my country, suffer persecution under the pressing-iron of reproach; or let my skin be punched full of eyelet-holes — holes for shoelaces — with the bodkin of derision."

Bodkins were used to pierce holes in cloth or leather.

Astley the legal clerk said, "I would sooner lose both my ears on the pillory of forgery."

A punishment for forgery was cropping the forger's ears.

Heron the textile dealer said, "Let me first live a bankrupt, and die in the lousy Hole of hunger, without settling with my creditors for sixpence in the pound."

The Counter was a prison in London for debtors, and the Hole was the place in that prison where the poorest prisoners were kept. Prisoners with some money could pay the jailers for better accommodations.

John a-Water the politician said, "If men fail not in their expectations, there may be spirits also that digest no rude affronts, Master Secretary Frion, or I am deceived, which is possible, I grant."

"Resolved like men of knowledge," Frion said, applauding their decision to put on a masque.

He continued, "At this feast, then, in honor of the bride, the Scots, I know, will in some show, some masque, or some other entertainment, present their homage. Now it would be uncomely if we were to be found less eager to perform for our prince than they are for their lady; and by how much we outshine them in the eyes of persons of account, by so much more will our endeavors meet with a livelier applause. Great emperors have for their recreations undertaken such kind of pastimes. As for the idea for the masque, refer it to my study; you all shall share thanks in the performance. It will be pleasurable."

Heron the textile dealer said, "The proposal is allowed. I have stolen away to a dancing school when I was an apprentice."

Astley the legal clerk said, "There have been noisy, tumultuous, Irish hubbubs when I have made an actor, too."

Skelton the tailor said, "As for fashioning of shapes and cutting a cross-caper in a dance, turn me off to my trade again."

A shape can be 1) an attitude in dancing, or 2) a costume. A cross-caper is a move in dancing, and it may be a reference to the traditional tailors' custom of working while sitting cross-legged.

John a-Water the politician said, "Surely there is, if I am not deceived, a kind of gravity in merriment; as there is, or perhaps ought to be, respect of persons in the quality of bearing, which is as it is construed, either so or so."

"Always you come home to me and understand my meaning," Frion said. "As opportunity arises I find you relish — taste and appreciate — court-conduct with discretion, and court-conduct and discretion are fit for statesmen of your merits. Please wait for the prince and in his ear acquaint him with this plan. I'll follow and direct you."

Everyone except Frion exited.

Alone, he said to himself, "Oh, the toil of humoring this abject scum of mankind, muddy-brained peasants! Princes feel a misery beyond impartial sufferance."

"Impartial sufferance" is the suffering that is dealt out impartially to members of the human species.

Frion continued, "Princes in extreme circumstances must yield to such abettors — yet now our tide runs smoothly, without adverse winds. Run on! Flow to a full sea! Time alone abates the quarrels that are forewritten in the Book of Fates."

As time goes on, our complaints and our grievances lessen in intensity.

CHAPTER 3

— 3.1 —

King Henry VII, wearing his gorget (armor protecting the throat) and carrying his sword, plume of feathers for his headgear, and truncheon (staff representing command), talked with Christopher Urswick in the palace at Westminster. On this day, 17 June 1497, King Henry VII's army would meet the Cornish rebels in the Battle of Deptford Bridge (also known as the Battle of Blackheath).

"How runs the time of day?" King Henry VII asked. "What time is it?"

"Past ten, my lord," Christopher Urswick answered.

"A bloody hour will it prove to some whose disobedience, like the sons of the earth, throws a defiance against the face of Heaven," King Henry VII said.

The sons of the earth were the mythological Giants, who rebelled — unsuccessfully — against the Olympian gods.

King Henry VII said, "Oxford, with Essex and brave De la Pole, have quieted the Londoners, I hope, and set them safe from fear."

King Henry VII had sent these men and their soldiers to oppose the rebels.

"The Londoners are all silent," Christopher Urswick said.

"From their own battlements — the city walls — they may behold the big open space of Saint George's fields overspread with armed men, among whom our own royal standard threatens destruction to opposers. We must learn to practice war again in time of peace, or lay our crown before our subjects' feet, Urswick, mustn't we?"

"The armed forces who seated King Henry VII — you — on his lawful throne will forever rise up in his defense," Christopher Urswick said.

"Rage and violence shall not frighten the bosom of our confidence," King Henry VII said. "Our Cornish rebels, deceived in their hopes of getting aid in Kent, met brave resistance there by that country's Earl, George Abergeny, and by Cobham, Poynings, Guilford, and other loyal hearts.

"Now, if Blackheath must be preserved in order to be the fatal tomb to swallow such stiff-necked, obstinate, downtrodden people as with weary marches have travelled from their homes, their wives, and children, to pay, instead of taxes, their lives, we may continue as sovereign. Yet, Urswick, we'll

48

not abate one penny of what in Parliament has freely been contributed; we must not. Money gives soul to action.

"Our competitor, the Flemish counterfeit, with King James IV of Scotland, will prove through experience what courage can be nourished by need and want, lacking the food of fit supplies."

King Henry VII believed that soon Perkin Warbeck would learn through experience that unsatisfied need and shortage of supplies take away courage. Well-equipped, well-nourished soldiers fight more courageously.

He continued, "But, Urswick, I have a secret charm that shall unloose the witchcraft wherewith young King James IV is bound, and free it at my pleasure without bloodshed."

Skilled at political maneuvering, King Henry VII was saying that he had a secret plan that would make King James IV of Scotland abandon Perkin Warbeck.

"Your majesty's a wise King sent from Heaven, the Protector of the just," Christopher Urswick replied.

"Let dinner cheerfully be served in," King Henry VII said. "This day of the week is ours, our day of providence; for Saturday has never yet failed in all my undertakings to yield me rest at night."

Saturday was his lucky day.

Trumpets sounded.

King Henry VII asked, "What is the meaning of this warning? Good fate, speak peace to Henry VII!"

Lord Chamberlain Giles Dawbeney, the Earl of Oxford, and some attendants entered the scene.

"Live the King, triumphant in the ruin of his enemies!" Lord Chamberlain Giles Dawbeney said.

"The head of strong rebellion is cut off, and the body hewed in pieces," the Earl of Oxford said.

"Giles Dawbeney, Oxford, favorites to noblest fortunes, how yet stands the comfort of your wishes?" King Henry VII asked. "What has happened in the battle?"

"Briefly thus," Lord Chamberlain Giles Dawbeney said. "The Cornish under Audley, disappointed in their exaggerated expectation of aid from the Kentish — who are your majesty's right-trusty liegemen and faithful subjects

— flew, feathered and winged by rage and heartened by presumption, to take the field even at your palace-gates, and face you in your royal chamber. Arrogance aggravated their ignorance; for they, supposing, misled by rumor, that the day of battle would fall on Monday, they instead defied your armed forces with bravado rather than feared any onset of battle."

King Henry VII had spread the rumor that he would attack on Monday; instead, he had attacked two days earlier, on Saturday.

Lord Chamberlain Giles Dawbeney continued, "Yet this morning, when in the dawning I, by your direction, strove to get Deptford-strand bridge, there I found such a resistance as might show what strength could make. Arrows hailed in showers upon us a full yard long at least, but we prevailed."

The arrows were shot from longbows.

He continued, "My Lord of Oxford circling round the hill with his fellow peers, fell fiercely on them on the one side, and I on the other, until, great sir — pardon my oversight — eager of doing some memorable act, I was engaged almost a prisoner, but was freed as soon as became sensible of danger."

He was unclear in his speech due to glossing over his error: He had attempted to do a notable deed on the battlefield, and almost became a prisoner (actually, he was briefly captured), but when he and/or other soldiers on his side became aware of the danger, he moved away from the danger (actually, the enemy freed him, perhaps because they were losing the battle and were hoping for clemency after the battle).

Lord Chamberlain Giles Dawbeney continued, "Now the fight began in heat, which was then quenched in the blood of two thousand rebels. As many more rebels are reserved to test your mercy — they are our prisoners. This battle has brought back a victory with safety."

"Have we lost a number of soldiers equal to the number the rebels lost?" King Henry VII asked.

"In the total we have lost scarcely four hundred," the Earl of Oxford said.

He added, "Audley, Flammock, and Joseph — the ringleaders of this rebellion — are tied up in a line in ropes, which are fit ornaments for traitors since ropes can be used as nooses. They await your sentencing."

King Henry VII said, "We must pay our thanks where they are alone due, to God and Heaven.

"Oh, lords, here is no victory, nor shall our people conceive that we can triumph in their falls. Alas, poor souls! Let such as have escaped steal back to the country without pursuit. There's not a drop of blood spilt but has drawn as much of mine; their swords could have wrought wonders on their King's part — their swords that half-heartily were unsheathed against their prince, but which wounded their own breasts.

"Lords, we are debtors to your care; our payment shall be both sure and befitting your merit."

Lord Chamberlain Giles Dawbeney asked, "Sir, will you please to see those rebels who were the heads and leaders of this wild monster-like multitude?"

King Henry VII replied, "Dear friend, my faithful Giles Dawbeney, no."

King Henry VII had been merciful to the common soldiers, but he would not be merciful to their leaders.

He continued, "On the leaders, our justice must frown in terror. I will not deign to cast an eye of pity on them. Let false, traitorous Audley be drawn upon a hurdle — a frame or sled — from the Newgate Prison to Tower Hill in his own coat of arms painted on paper, with the arms reversed, defaced and torn; there let him lose his head."

Nobles such as Lord Audley were beheaded after being found guilty of treason. Commoners suffered different fates.

King Henry VII continued, "The lawyer and the blacksmith shall be hanged and cut into four quarters; their quarters shall be sent into Cornwall to be examples to the rest, whom we are pleased to pardon and dismiss from further pursuit and from further judicial inquiry."

He then ordered, "My Lord of Oxford, see that it is done."

"I shall, sir," the Earl of Oxford replied.

"Urswick!" King Henry VII said.

"My lord?" he replied.

"Say to Dinham, our High Treasurer, that we command commissions be newly granted for the collection of our taxes through all the west, and that very speedily."

He was sending tax collectors to Cornwall.

King Henry VII then said, "Lords, we acknowledge our obligations due for your most constant and loyal services."

Lord Chamberlain Giles Dawbeney gave credit where credit was due — the common soldiers had fought well: "Your soldiers have manfully and faithfully acquitted their several and individual duties."

"And for it we will throw a largess — a gift of money — freely among them, which shall hearten and encourage their loyalties," King Henry VII said. "More yet remains of this kind of employment; not a man can be dismissed until our enemies abroad — Perkin Warbeck and his supporters — who are more dangerous than these at home, have felt the puissance and force of our arms.

"Oh, happy are the Kings whose thrones are raised in their subjects' hearts!"

— 3.2 —

The Earl of Huntley and Lord Dalyell talked together in the palace at Edinburgh. The wedding of Perkin Warbeck and Lady Katherine was being celebrated.

The Earl of Huntley and Lord Dalyell were both unhappy, but only the Earl of Huntley was putting on a grotesque imitation of a happy man.

"Now, sir, a modest word with you, sad gentleman," the Earl of Huntley said to Lord Dalyell. "Isn't this fine, I suppose, to see the gambols, hear the jigs, observe the frisks, be enchanted with the excellent discord of bells, pipes, and the small drums called tabors and the confused hotch-potch of Scotch and Irish twingling-twangling harpists, which are similar to so many insane choristers at Bedlam Hospital singing a round of a song!

"The feasts, the manly, hearty appetites, the pledging of healths in usquebaugh, aka whisky, and bonny-clabber, aka beer and buttermilk, the ale in dishes never fetched from China, the hundred-thousand delicacies not to be spoken of — and all this for King Oberon and Queen Mab of the fairies — should put a soul into you."

Perkin Warbeck and Lady Katherine were figuratively King Oberon and Queen Mab of the fairies.

The Earl of Huntley continued, "Look, good man, how youthful I am grown, but if you don't mind my saying so, this new Queen-bride must henceforth be no more my daughter — no, by our lady, it is unfit.

"And yet you see how I bear this change. I think I do so courageously, and so you should then shake off your cares and worries in such a time of jollity."

"Alas, sir," Lord Dalyell replied, "how can you cast a mist upon and cover up your griefs?

"Your griefs, howsoever you conceal them in shadow, still present to any judging eye the perfect substance of grief, of which my griefs are but counterfeits."

"Bah, Dalyell!" the Earl of Huntley said. "Thou interrupt the part I bear in music to this rare bridal-feast. Let us be merry, while flattering calms make us feel overconfident about storms. Tempests, when they begin to roar, put out the light of peace and cloud the sun's bright eye in darkness of despair; as of right now, we are safe."

Mist, which is less dense than fog, conceals grief, but a tempest blots out the sun and causes grief. A light mistiness in the eyes can conceal grief, but a tempest of tears reveals grief.

"I wish you could as easily forget the justice of your sorrows as my hopes can yield to destiny," Lord Dalyell said.

"Bah!" the Earl of Huntley said. "Then I see thou do not know the flexible condition of my apt — and aped — nature."

His nature was apt in that it could adapt to bad conditions — or so he claimed. It was aped in that it was imitative: He did not feel happy, but he was imitating — badly — a happy man.

The Earl of Huntley continued:

"I can laugh, laugh heartily, when the gout cramps my joints.

"Just let the kidney stone stop in my bladder, and I am immediately singing.

"The quartan-fever that strikes every fourth day, shrinking every limb, sets me capering and dancing right away.

"Betray me, and you bind me as a friend forever.

"Indeed, I trust that the losing of a daughter, although I doted on every hair that grew to trim her head, does not allow the presence of any pain like one of these.

"Come, thou are deceived in me when you think that I feel pain and grief.

"Give me a blow, a sound blow on the face, and I'll thank thee for it.

"I love the wrongs that are done to me. Thou are deceived in me if you think that I do not."

He was saying that he felt no pain and no grief.

It was more accurate, however, to say that no other pain and grief could compare to the pain and grief of losing his daughter. The pain and grief of losing his daughter made every other pain and grief seem pleasurable.

"Deceived!" Lord Dalyell said. "Oh, noble Huntley, my few years have learnt experience of too ripe an age to forfeit fit credulity. I know what is believable and what is unbelievable.

"I do not believe that you feel no pain and no grief.

"Forgive my rudeness; I am bold."

He was rude and bold because he was calling the Earl of Huntley — an older man — a liar.

The Earl of Huntley said, "Forgive me first a madness of ambition.

"Through your example teach me humility, for patience and calmness scorn lectures, which schoolmen are accustomed to read to boys who are incapable of injuries."

Schoolboys are too young to have daughters old enough to be married to an impostor by the King, and so they are incapable of being injured by such a deed.

In order to learn how to deal with such a bad situation as this, it would take the example of another person. Simply hearing advice about how to deal with such a calamity is worthless. In such a bad situation, the positive example of someone with experience is much more worthwhile.

The Earl of Huntley continued, "Although I am old, I could grow tough in fury, and disclaim allegiance to my King. I could fall at odds with all my fellow peers who dared not stand up as defenders against the rape done on my honor.

"But Kings are earthly gods, so there is no meddling with their anointed bodies; as for their actions, Kings are accountable only to Heaven.

"Yet in the puzzle of my troubled brain, one antidote's kept in reserve against the poison of my temporary madness; it lies in thee to apply the antidote."

"Name it," Lord Dalyell said. "Oh, name it quickly, sir! Tell me what the antidote is!"

"The antidote is a pardon for my most foolish slighting thy deserts; I have culled out this time to beg your pardon. Please, be generous; had I been so, thou had owned a happy bride, but now she is a castaway, and she is never a child of mine anymore."

The Earl of Huntley now regretted not using his power as a father to make his daughter marry Lord Dalyell, and he was begging Lord Dalyell to forgive him. Because the Earl of Huntley had been ambitious for a socially reputable marriage for his daughter, he had missed the opportunity to have her married to a good man: Lord Dalyell.

"Don't say that, sir," Lord Dalyell said. "Lady Katherine is not at fault here."

"The world would prate about how she was beautiful," the Earl of Huntley said. "I know she was young, tender, and sweet in her obedience. But she is lost now. What a bankrupt am I now, fallen from a full stock of blessings!

"Must I hope for a mercy from thy heart?"

"You shall receive it," Lord Dalyell said. "You shall receive a love, a service, and a friendship to posterity."

"May good angels reward thy charity!" the Earl of Huntley replied. "I have nothing more except prayers left to me now."

"I'll lend you mirth, sir, if you will be in harmony with me and with yourself," Lord Dalyell said.

No such mirth would be forthcoming. Such harmony was not possible at this time. At best, they could endure their sorrow together.

"Thank you truly," the Earl of Huntley said. "I must; yes, yes, I must.

"Here's yet some ease: a partner in affliction. Do not look angry."

"Good, noble sir!" Lord Dalyell said.

He was not angry; instead, he felt pity.

Trumpets sounded.

"Oh, listen!" the Earl of Huntley said. "We must be quiet. The King and all the others are coming.

"Here is a meeting of festive sights. This day is the last of the revels.

"Tomorrow sounds of war; then we will see a new exchange: Fiddles must turn to swords.

"Unhappy marriage!"

Trumpets again sounded.

King James IV, Perkin Warbeck and Lady Katherine, the Earl of Crawford and his Countess, and Jane Douglas and other ladies entered the scene.

The Earl of Huntley and Lord Dalyell fell in among them.

King James IV said to Perkin Warbeck, "Cousin of York, you and your princely bride have liberally enjoyed such soft delights as a new-married couple could anticipate, nor has our generosity shorted expectation. But after all those pleasures of repose, of amorous safety, we must rouse the ease of dalliance with achievements of more glory than sloth and sleep can furnish; yet, for farewell, we gladly entertain a truce with time in order to grace the joint endeavors of our servants."

Perkin Warbeck replied, "My royal cousin, in your princely favor the extent of bounty has been so unlimited that an acknowledgment in words only would breed suspicion of our state and quality. When we shall, in the fullness of our Fate — completed by its minister, Necessity — sit on our own throne as King of England, then our arms, laid open in gratitude, in sacred memory of these large benefits, shall entwine our benefactors closely, even to our thoughts and heart, without distinction. Then James IV and Richard IV, being in effect one person, shall unite and rule one people, divisible in titles only."

Perkin Warbeck was saying that he would thank King James IV of Scotland with more than words when he became King Richard IV of England. His thanks would include peace between England and Scotland and a close relationship with King James IV of Scotland.

"Be seated," King James IV said.

He then asked, "Are the performers ready?"

"All are entering," the Earl of Crawford replied.

"Dainty entertainment is approaching, Dalyell!" the Earl of Huntley said. "Sit; come, sit. Sit and be quiet; here are kingly bug's-words!"

Bug's-words were the pompous, overly courtly words that the Earl of Huntley expected to be spoken by Perkin Warbeck.

Four grotesque performers costumed as Scotchmen entered through one door. Warbeck's followers, costumed as four long-haired wild Irishmen in trousers, entered through another door.

Music played, and the performers danced.

"To all a general thanks!" King James IV said.

"In the next room put on your own clothing again; you shall receive the particular and individual acknowledgment of a gift of money," Perkin Warbeck said.

The performers exited.

"Enough of merriments," King James IV said.

He then asked, "Crawford, how far's our army upon the march?"

"The soldiers are at Hedonhall, great King," the Earl of Crawford answered. "They number twelve thousand well-prepared soldiers."

"Crawford, tonight travel there posthaste," King James IV said. "We in person, with the prince, by four o'clock tomorrow after dinner will be with you; speed away!"

"I fly, my lord," the Earl of Crawford said, and then he exited.

"Our business grows to a head — a critical point — now," King James IV said to Perkin Warbeck. "Where's Frion, your secretary? Why isn't he present to serve you?"

"He is with Marchmont, your herald," Perkin Warbeck replied.

"Good," King James IV said. "The proclamation's ready. By that it will appear how the English feel about your title."

The purpose of the proclamation was to announce publicly to the English that their true King — Perkin Warbeck — was coming. The reaction to the proclamation would help King James IV and Perkin Warbeck gauge the English reaction to Perkin Warbeck: Did they support him or not?

"Huntley, comfort your daughter in her husband's absence," King James IV said. "Fight with prayers at home for us, who for your honors must toil in fight abroad."

"Prayers are the weapons that men so near their graves as I am use," the Earl of Huntley said. "I've little else to do."

"To rest, young beauties!" King James IV said.

He added, "We must be early stirring; we must quickly part. A kingdom's rescue craves both speed and art."

The kingdom being "rescued" and returned to its "true King" was England.

"Art" in this context meant "skill and cunning."

"Cousins, goodnight," King James IV said to Perkin Warbeck and Lady Katherine.

"We wish rest to our cousin-King," Perkin Warbeck said.

"Your blessing, sir," Lady Katherine said to her father.

The Earl of Huntley said, "Fair blessings on your highness! To be sure, you need them."

Everyone except Perkin Warbeck, Lady Katherine, and Jane Douglas exited.

"Jane, set the lights down, and from us give to the performers in the next room this little purse of money," Perkin Warbeck said, giving her money. "Tell them that we'll deserve their loves."

Jane Douglas replied, "It shall be done, sir," and then she exited.

Now Perkin Warbeck and his new wife, Lady Katherine, were alone.

He said, "Now, dearest, before sweet sleep shall seal your eyes, which are love's precious taper — lights — give me permission to engage in a parting ceremony now; for tomorrow it would be sacrilege to intrude upon the temple of thy peace. Swift as the morning I must break from the soft down of thy embraces in order to put on hard steel and tread the paths that lead through various hazards to a full-of-worries throne."

"Down" consists of the soft feathers of a bird. Lady Katherine's embraces were soft.

"My lord, I'd be delighted to go with you," Lady Katherine said. "There's little benefit in staying behind here."

"The churlish brow of war, fair dearest, is a sight of horror when it comes to ladies' entertainment," Perkin Warbeck said.

He did not want her to witness war.

He continued, "If thou should hear a report of my sad ending by the hand of some English subject who against nature fights against his true King, thou in addition shall hear how I died worthy of my right to the crown by falling like a King; and in the close of my life, my last breath shall sound this cadence: thy name.

"Thy name, thou fairest, shall sing a requiem to my soul, unwilling to move on only to greater glory, because in the Heavenly Paradise it will be divided from such a Heaven on Earth as life with thee.

"But these are chimes for funerals. My business now turns to fortune of a sprightlier triumph: For love and majesty are reconciled, and both of them vow to crown thee Empress of the west."

"You have a noble language, sir," Lady Katherine said. "Your right in me is without question, and however events of time may shorten my deservings of others' pity, yet it shall not stagger and daunt either constancy or duty in a wife."

Events could quickly make her deserving of others' pity if her husband were to soon die on the battlefield.

She concluded, "You must be King of me; and my poor heart is all I can call mine."

"But we will live, live, beauteous virtue, by the living proof of our own blood, to let the counterfeit be known as the world's object of contempt," Perkin Warbeck said.

He meant the word "counterfeit" to mean King Henry VII, but it probably more accurately referred to himself.

"Please, do not use that word," Lady Katherine said. "It carries fate in it."

She added, "I now make the first request I ever made to you, and I trust that your love for me will grant it."

"I will make no denial, dearest."

"My request is that hereafter, if you return safely, no adventure may sever us in tasting and experiencing any fortune," Lady Katherine said. "I never can stay behind again."

"You're lady of your desires, and you shall command whatever you will," Perkin Warbeck said. "Yet it is too hard to promise."

"What our destinies have decreed in their books we must not probe and examine, but kneel to," Lady Katherine said. "We must accept what is written in the Book of Fate."

"Then to fear when hope is fruitless would be to be desperately miserable," Perkin Warbeck said. "This poverty of spirit our greatness dares not dream of, and much more our greatness scorns to stoop to.

"Some few minutes remain yet before I go; let's be thriving and successful in our hopes."

— 3.3 —

King Henry VII, Pedro Hialas, and Christopher Urswick talked together in the palace at Westminster.

Many countries took an interest in the King Henry VII-Perkin Warbeck conflict. France had invaded Italy; and now Spain, Venice, and the Holy Roman Emperor hoped that King Henry VII of England would join them in their opposition to France. In addition, King Ferdinand and Queen Isabella of Spain were hoping to marry their daughter Katherine of Aragon to Prince Arthur, King Henry VII's oldest son. Because of that, they wanted Henry VII to keep his crown.

"Your name is Pedro Hialas, and you are a Spaniard?" King Henry VII asked.

"Sir, I am a Castilian born," he replied.

In 1469, Ferdinand married Isabella. He was the heir to the King of Aragon, and in 1469 she became the Queen of Castile. In 1479, Ferdinand's father died, and the two kingdoms became unified and Ferdinand and Isabella became the first monarchs to rule a unified Spain. Queen Isabella I of Castile and King Ferdinand II of Aragon are collectively known in history as the Catholic Monarchs.

"King Ferdinand and wise Queen Isabel, his royal consort, have written that you are a man worthy of trust and candor. Heaven holds dear princes who meet with subjects who are sincere in their employments. Your recommendation, sir, declares you to be such a subject.

"Let me declare how joyful I consider the amity and friendship I have with your most fortunate master, who almost seems to have experienced a miracle in his success against the Moors, who had devoured his country, but which is now entirely under the control of his scepter."

In 1492, Spain became completely under the rule of Ferdinand and Isabella.

King Henry VII continued, "We, for our part, will imitate his foresight in governing, in hope of sharing in his success in governing.

"We attribute the secrecy of his advice to us by you, who are intended to be an ambassador to Scotland, to create a peace between our kingdoms, to be a policy of love, which well becomes His wisdom and our care."

Pedro Hialas was being sent to Scotland in an attempt to turn King James IV against Perkin Warbeck, but he had first stopped to secretly meet with King Henry VII, a secret meeting that Henry VII told Pedro Hialas that he attributed to King Ferdinand's concern for him and for the two Kingdoms.

"Your majesty understands him rightly," Pedro Hialas said.

King Henry VII replied, "If not, your knowledge can instruct me, wherein, sir, to have recourse to ceremony would seem useless, which we shall not need, for I will be as studious of your concealment in our secret meeting as any council shall advise. I will be very careful not to reveal that we have met."

Any kind of ceremony would make public Pedro Hialas' visit to the court of King James IV.

"Then, sir, my chief request is that on notice sent by me when I am in Scotland, you will send some learned man of power and experience to join in negotiations with me," Pedro Hialas said.

"I shall do it, being that way well provided by a servant who may attend you always," King Henry VII said.

Events would show that the servant would be Richard Fox, the Bishop of Durham.

Pedro Hialas said, "If King James IV of Scotland, by any roundabout or devious means, should perceive my coming near your court, I fear the outcome of my employment. I am afraid that if King James IV knows that I have met with you, then my negotiations with him will fail."

"Don't be your own herald," King Henry VII said. "I learn sometimes without a teacher."

He meant that he already understood the need for secrecy: It was obvious.

"May good days guard all your princely thoughts!" Pedro Hialas said.

King Henry VII ordered, "Urswick, accompany him no further than the nearest public corridor."

This would help keep Pedro Hialas' visit to the court secret.

He then said to Pedro Hialas, "A hearty love go with you!"

"I am your vowed beadsman," Pedro Hialas said.

A beadsman is a person who is paid to pray for another person. Pedro Hialas was saying that he was King Henry VII's humble servant.

Christopher Urswick and Pedro Hialas exited.

"King Ferdinand is not so much a fox but that a cunning huntsman may in time fall on the scent," King Henry VII said to himself. "In honorable actions safe, free-from-risk imitation best deserves a praise."

Christopher Urswick returned, and King Henry VII asked, "Has the Castilian departed?"

"He has, and secretly — without his presence being known," Christopher Urswick replied. "The two hundred marks your majesty conveyed to him, he gently pocketed with a very modest gravity."

"What was it he muttered in the earnest of his wisdom?" King Henry VII said. "He spoke not to be heard; it was about ...?"

"Warbeck," Christopher Urswick answered. "How if you, King Henry VII, were only assured of the loyalty of your subjects, such a wild vagabond as Perkin Warbeck might soon be caged, with no great ado arising against his caging."

"Nay, nay," King Henry VII said. "He said something about my son Prince Arthur's marriage match."

"Right, right, sir," Christopher Urswick replied. "He hummed and hawed it out, how that King Ferdinand swore that the marriage between the Lady Katherine of Aragon, his daughter, and the Prince of Wales, your son Arthur, should never be consummated as long as any Earl of Warwick lived in England, except by new creation."

Edward, Earl of Warwick, was the only surviving son of George, Earl of Clarence, the brother of King Edward IV and King Richard III.

Edward, Earl of Warwick, was first cousin to King Edward V, one of the two Princes of the Tower of London who vanished in 1483, presumed murdered by their uncle, Duke Richard of York, who became King Richard III.

The Earl of Clarence was King Edward IV's and King Richard III's brother; therefore, many people considered Edward, Earl of Warwick, to have a better claim to the throne of England than King Henry VII. Because of this, King Ferdinand and Queen Isabella were leery about marrying their daughter Katherine of Aragon to King Henry VII's oldest son, Arthur. The Spanish monarchs wanted to be sure that King Henry VII's grasp on the English crown was secure; one way to help that happen would be if Edward, Earl of Warwick, were dead and another, newly created Earl of Warwick took his place.

Of course, King Ferdinand and Queen Isabella were also concerned about King James IV's support for Perkin Warbeck. They had sent Pedro Hialas to Scotland to convince King James IV to abandon his support of Warbeck.

"I remember it was so, indeed," King Henry VII said. "The King his master swore it?"

"That is exactly what he said," Christopher Urswick said.

"An Earl of Warwick!" King Henry VII said.

King Henry VII was quick to make decisions; he knew that it was important to convince King James IV of Scotland to abandon his support for Perkin Warbeck.

He ordered, "Provide a messenger for letters instantly for Richard Fox, Bishop of Durham."

The Bishop of Durham was in the north of England, preparing the border castle at Norham to resist the coming Scottish invasion.

King Henry VII added, "Our news from Scotland creeps. It comes so slowly that we must have spirits that travel quickly through the air rather than slowly on land. Our time requires dispatch."

He then said to himself, "The Earl of Warwick! Let him be son to the Earl of Clarence, younger brother to Edward! Edward's daughter is, I think, mother to our Prince Arthur."

Prince Arthur was a grandson to King Edward IV, as was the Earl of Warwick. Prince Arthur's relationship to King Edward IV was more direct than the Earl of Warwick's, but Prince Arthur's relationship to King Edward IV came through the female line, while the Earl of Warwick's relationship to King Edward IV came through the male line.

Prince Arthur's parents were King Henry VII and Elizabeth of York, daughter of King Edward IV.

The Earl of Warwick's father was the Duke of Clarence, brother of King Edward IV and King Richard III.

King Henry VII ordered, "Get a messenger."

— 3.4 —

King James IV of Scotland, Perkin Warbeck, the Earl of Crawford, Lord Dalyell, Heron, Astley, John a-Water, and Skelton met before the castle of Norham. Some soldiers were present.

King James IV and the others were besieging the castle of Norham. Inside the castle was the Bishop of Durham, who was defending it.

Norham Castle is located on the River Tweed, part of which is traditionally the boundary between England and Scotland.

"We waste time against these castle walls," King James IV of Scotland said. "The English prelate will not surrender. Give him a summons once more."

A trumpet sounded a distinctive call to request a meeting between the two sides.

Wearing armor, the Bishop of Durham appeared on the walls of the castle, holding a truncheon that represented command in his hand. Some English soldiers appeared with him.

"Look, the jolly clergyman appears, dressed like a ruffian!" Perkin Warbeck said.

King James IV said, "Bishop of Durham, yet set open the castle gates, and to your lawful sovereign, Richard of York — Perkin Warbeck — surrender this castle, and he will take thee to his grace. Otherwise, the Tweed River shall overflow its banks with English blood, and wash the sand that cements those hard stones from their foundation."

The Bishop of Durham ignored Perkin Warbeck as he said, "Warlike King of Scotland, permit a few words from a man forced to lay his Bible aside, and clap on armor and weapons unsuitable to my age or my profession.

"Courageous prince, consider on what grounds you rend the face of peace, and break a league with an allied King — Henry VII — who courts your amity and friendship. And for whom do you do this? For a vagabond, a straggler, not noted in the world by birth or name, an obscure peasant, by the rage of hell loosed from his chains to set great Kings at strife.

"What nobleman, what common man of note, what ordinary subject has come in to join your side, since first you set foot on our territories, to even pretend you have a welcome?

"Children laugh at your proclamations, and the wiser people pity so great a potentate's being taken advantage of by one who deceives completely with the fawning behavior and newness of an instructed compliment — he had to be taught how to act toward royalty rather than learning naturally through being born royal.

"Such spoils, such slaughters as the rapine of your soldiers already have committed, is enough to show your zeal in an imagined just cause. Yet, great King, don't wake my master's vengeance but instead shake off that viper that gnaws your entrails."

This society believed that the offspring of vipers gnawed their way out of their mother's body. Vipers were symbols of ingratitude.

The Bishop of Durham continued, "I and my fellow-subjects are resolved, if you persist, to withstand your utmost fury until our last drop of blood falls from us."

Perkin Warbeck said to King James IV, "Oh, sir, lend no ear to this traducer and slanderer of my honor!"

He said to the Bishop of Durham, "What shall I call thee, thou gray-bearded scandal, who kicks against the sovereign — me — to whom thou owes allegiance?"

He then said to King James IV, "Treason is bold-faced and eloquent in mischief. Sacred King, be deaf to his known malice."

The Bishop of Durham continued to ignore Perkin Warbeck as he said to King James IV, "Rather yield to those holy impulses that inspire the sacred heart of an anointed body."

During their coronations, Kings were anointed with oil.

He continued, "It is the surest policy in princes to govern well their own than seek encroachment upon another's right."

King James IV of Scotland thought hard.

"The King is serious, deep in his thoughts," the Earl of Crawford said quietly to Lord Dalyell.

"May his better genius lift his thoughts up to Heaven!" Lord Dalyell replied quietly.

A genius is a protective spirit: a guardian angel.

"Can you ponder while such a devil raves?" Perkin Warbeck said. "Oh, sir!"

"Well, bishop, you'll not be drawn to mercy?" King James IV asked.

"Construe me in like case by a subject of your own," the Bishop of Durham said. "I am acting as you would expect one of your own subjects to act in a similar situation.

"My resolution's fixed. I will remain loyal to my King: Henry VII.

"King James IV, be advised: A greater fate waits on thee. You were born to do better and greater things than this."

The Bishop of Durham and his soldiers exited from the walls.

King James IV of Scotland said, "Plunder through the country; spare no prey of life or goods."

"Oh, sir, then give me leave to yield to natural feelings and weep," Perkin Warbeck said. "I am most miserable. Had I been born what this clergyman would by defamation baffle and confound belief with, I would have never sought the truth of my inheritance with women raped, infants murdered, virgins deflowered, old men butchered, dwellings fired, my land depopulated, and my people afflicted with a kingdom's devastation! Show more pity, great King, or I shall never endure to see such havoc with dry eyes. Spare, spare, my dear, dear England!"

King James IV replied, "You make your piety foolish by being ridiculously anxious about an interest another man possesses. Where's your faction? Where are your supporters? Shrewdly the Bishop of Durham guessed the 'support' of your adherents. When not a citizen of some town, no, not a villager has yet appeared in your assistance, that should make you whine, and not your country's suffering, as you term it."

Not one Englishman had come out to support Perkin Warbeck's claim to the throne of England.

"The King is angry," Lord Dalyell said.

"And the overly emotional Duke is effeminately grieving," the Earl of Crawford replied.

Perkin Warbeck said, "The experience in former trials, sir, both of my own or of other princes cast out of their thrones, have so acquainted me with how misery is destitute of friends or of relief, that I can easily submit to taste and experience the lowest reproof — the basest ignominy — without contempt or angry words."

"A humble-minded man!" King James IV said sarcastically.

Frion entered the scene.

King James IV asked him, "Now, what news does Master Secretary Frion bring?"

"King Henry VII of England has in open field overthrown the armies of the Cornish rebels who opposed him in the right of this young prince: Perkin Warbeck," Frion said.

"His taxes, you mean," King James IV said.

He knew that the Cornish rebels had not risen up in support of Perkin Warbeck's claim to the throne, but rather they had rebelled because of excessive taxation.

"Do you have more news?" King James IV asked.

"Howard, Earl of Surrey, backed by twelve earls and barons of the north, a hundred knights and gentlemen of name, and twenty thousand soldiers, is at hand to raise your siege. Baron Willoughby de Broke, with a splendid navy, is admiral at sea; and Giles Dawbeney follows with an intact and undefeated army in support."

"That is false!" Perkin Warbeck said. "They come to side with us."

King James IV immediately showed that he did not believe Perkin Warbeck.

"Retreat," he ordered. "We shall not find them stones and walls to cope with. Fighting them will be more difficult than laying siege to a castle."

He then said to Perkin Warbeck, "Yet, Duke of York, for such thou say thou are, I'll try thy fortune to the height: I will test your luck to the utmost."

Previously, King James IV had used the respectful "you" when talking to Perkin Warbeck; now he used the less respectful "thou." Previously, King James IV had shown that he believed that Perkin Warbeck was the Duke of York; now he said, "Duke of York, for such thou say thou are."

King James IV of Scotland added, "By my herald Marchmont, I will send a brave challenge for single combat between the Earl of Surrey and me; for once a King will risk his person fighting against an Earl, with the condition of spilling less blood: The soldiers will not fight and shed their blood. Surrey is bold, and James IV is resolved."

"Oh, rather, gracious sir, advance me to this glory and give me the honor of fighting the single combat, since my cause is involved in this fair quarrel," Perkin Warbeck said. "Even valued at the least, I am King Henry VII's equal."

"I will be the man," King James IV said.

He then ordered, "March quietly off.

"Where victory can reap a harvest crowned with triumph, toil is cheap."

CHAPTER 4

— 4.1 —

The Earl of Surrey talked with the Bishop of Durham in the English military camp near Ayton, on the Borders. Some soldiers, with drums and colors, were present. King James IV of Scotland had made a raid into England, and so the Earl of Surrey had in response made a raid into Scotland.

They were at the Old Ayton Castle, which had been just demolished.

"Are all our boasting and defying enemies shrunk back, hidden in the fogs of their distempered climate, not daring to see our colors wave in hatred of this intemperate air?" the Earl of Surrey asked.

He then listed a number of Scottish castles that he had overthrown: "Can they look on the strength of Cundrestine defaced? The glory of Hedonhall devastated? That of Edington cast down? The Pile — small castle — of Fulden overthrown? And this the strongest of their forts, Old Ayton Castle, yielded and demolished?"

He continued, "And yet they do not peep abroad? The Scots are bold and hardy in battle, but it seems the cause they undertake, considered, appears unjointed in the frame of it."

In other words, Perkin Warbeck's cause wasn't worth fighting for.

The Bishop of Durham said, "Noble Surrey, our royal master's wisdom is at all times his fortune's harbinger: His wise decisions lead to his success and good fortune. For when he draws his sword to threaten war, his providence and foresight settle on peace, the crowning — the fulfillment — of an empire."

A trumpet sounded.

"Put the ranks of soldiers in order," the Earl of Surrey commanded. "It is a herald's sound: The herald carries some message from King James IV. Keep a fixed station."

Marchmont and another Scottish herald arrived. They were wearing sleeveless coats that were traditional garb for heralds.

"From Scotland's awe-inspiring majesty we come to the English general," Marchmont said.

"To me?" the Earl of Surrey said. "Say on."

"This is my message, then," Marchmont said. "Because the waste and prodigal effusion of so much guiltless blood as two powerful armies fighting must necessarily glut the earth's dry womb, King James IV's sweet compassion has found a way to prevent that bloodshed. Thus he says to thee, great Earl of Surrey, that in a single fight he offers his own royal person, fairly proposing only these conditions. First, that if victory settles our master's right, the Earl shall deliver for his ransom the town of Berwick to him, with the fishgarths."

Berwick was located on the Tweed River; both Scotland and England wanted control of this strategic town.

A garth is an enclosure. A fishgarth is an enclosure in a river or sea that keeps fish in an area where they can easily be caught. The fishgarth at Berwick was for salmon.

Marchmont continued, "Second, if Surrey shall prevail, then King James IV will pay a thousand pounds down immediately for his freedom, and silence further arms and not engage in battles. So speaks King James."

The single combat need not end in death.

"'So speaks King James'!" the Earl of Surrey said. "So like a King he speaks. Heralds, the English general returns a deeply felt devotion from his heart, his very soul, to this unequalled grace."

King James IV was offering to meet in single combat a mere Earl. Normally, Kings would offer to fight in single combat only other Kings, so this was an honor to the Earl of Surrey.

The Earl of Surrey continued, "For let the King know, noble heralds, truly, how his descent from his great throne, to honor a foreign subject with so high a title as his compeer and fellow in arms, has conquered me more than any sword could do; for which — my loyalty excepted and adhered to — I will serve his virtues ever in all humility.

"But tell him that Berwick is not mine to part with; in affairs of princes subjects cannot traffic in rights inherent to the crown. My life is mine, and that life I dare to freely risk, and — with pardon to some unbribed vainglory — if his majesty shall taste a change of fate, his liberty shall meet no articles. He will be set at liberty with no conditions made."

The "change of fate" that King James IV could suffer would be losing to the Earl of Surrey, who was respectful enough to James IV in his speech not to say that openly. He, of course, did say that indirectly — not even the "bribe" of the honor of a King's offering to meet him in single fight was enough to keep him from saying that.

He continued, "If I fall, falling so splendidly to a King, I refer me to his pleasure without condition."

If the Earl of Surrey would win the single combat, he would release King James IV without making any conditions for his release. If King James IV would win the single combat, he could do what he wanted with the Earl of Surrey.

The Earl of Surrey continued, "And for this dear favor, say that if I am not countermanded by my King, Henry VII, I will cease hostilities, unless provoked."

Marchmont replied, "This answer we shall relate to our King impartially."

The Bishop of Durham said, "I beg your pardon. Please do me the favor of having a little patience. Wait a moment, please."

He then said quietly to the Earl of Surrey, "Sir, you find by these gay flourishes how wearied travail makes one desire a willing rest; here's but a prologue, however confidently uttered, meant for some ensuing acts of peace.

"Consider the time of year, unseasonableness of weather, expense, and barrenness of profit; and an opportunity presents itself for an honorable treaty, which we may make good use of. I will go back, sent from you in point of noble gratitude, to King James, with these his heralds. You shall shortly hear from me, my lord, with orders either for continuing to take a break from war or for proceeding to fight against Scotland. King Henry VII, fear not, will be thankful for this service."

The Earl of Surrey replied quietly to the Bishop of Durham, "To your wisdom, Lord Bishop, I refer it. Do as you wish to do."

"Be it so, then," the Bishop of Durham replied quietly.

The Earl of Surrey said loudly, "Heralds, accept this chain and these few crowns."

Tradition required that heralds and messengers receive gifts. The chain was made of gold or silver.

Marchmont said, "We offer you our duty, noble general."

The Bishop of Durham said, "In partial repayment for such princely love, my lord the general is pleased to show the King your master his sincerest zeal with further treaty negotiations by no common man: I myself will return with you to your King James IV."

The Earl of Surrey said, "You bind my most faithful affections to you, Lord Bishop."

Marchmont said, "May all happiness attend your lordship!"

The Bishop of Durham and the heralds exited.

The Earl of Surrey said, "Come, friends and fellow-soldiers. We, I suspect, shall meet no enemies but woods and hills to fight with, so then it would be as good to feed and sleep at home. We may be free from danger without being carelessly overconfident."

— 4.2 —

Perkin Warbeck and Frion talked together.

"Frion, oh, Frion, all my hopes of glory are at a standstill! The Scottish King grows dull in purpose, frosty, and wayward, since this Spanish agent, Pedro Hialas, has mixed discourses with him; they are often in private conference together. I am not called to council now — may ruin fall on all Hialas' crafty shrugs of the shoulders! I feel that the edifice of my plans is tottering."

Frion said about King Henry VII, "Henry's policies stir with too many plots and snares."

Perkin Warbeck replied, "Let his mines filled with explosives, shaped in the bowels of the earth, blow up works raised for my defense, yet they never can toss into air the freedom of my birth, or deny that my blood is Plantagenet's: I am my father's son still.

"But, oh, Frion, when I bring into reckoning with my disasters my wife's co-partnership, my Kate's, my life's, then, then my frailty — my body — feels like an earthquake.

"May evil damn Henry's plots! Either I will be England's King, or let my aunt Margaret of Burgundy report my fall in the attempt rightfully deserved by our ancestors!"

Perkin Warbeck continued to not refer to Henry Tudor as King Henry VII of England.

"You grow too wild in emotion," Frion said. "If you will appear to be a prince indeed, confine your emotion to moderation."

This society believed that Kings and nobles should keep their emotions under control.

"What a saucy rudeness prompts this distrust!" Perkin Warbeck said. "If? If I will appear! Appear a prince!"

His point was that he *was* a prince and not imitating one.

He continued, "May Death throttle such deceits even in their birth of utterance! Cursed deceit of trust! We deceive ourselves by trusting others!

"You make me mad. It would be best, it seems, that I should turn impostor to myself, be my own counterfeit, belie the truth of my dear mother's womb, the sacred bed of a prince murdered and a living prince disgraced and treated badly!"

Perkin Warbeck was referring to the two princes in the Tower of London. According to him, one prince — King Edward V — was murdered, and the other prince — the Duke of York, aka Perkin Warbeck himself — survived but was being kept from his rightful place on the throne of England.

"Nay, if you have no ears to hear," Frion said, "I have no breath to spend in vain."

"Sir, sir, take heed!" Perkin Warbeck said. "Gold and the promise of promotion rarely fail in temptation."

He was accusing Frion of being bribed to lack loyalty to him.

"Why are you saying this to me?" Frion asked.

"I mean nothing by saying it," Perkin Warbeck said, calming down. "Speak what you will; we are not sunk so low but that your advice may piece together again the heart that many cares have broken. You have been accustomed in all extremities to talk of comfort; have you no comfort for me left now? I'll not interrupt you.

"Good sir, bear with my mental disturbances! If King James should deny us dwelling here, whither must I go next? I ask you not to be angry."

Frion replied, "Sir, I told you about letters that have come from Ireland, telling how the Cornish resent their last defeat by the armies of Henry, and the Cornish humbly request that you would in person, with such forces as you could raise, land in Cornwall, where thousands will gladly maintain your title."

Perkin Warbeck now used the familiar "thee" and "thou" used by close friends in referring to Frion rather than the formal "you":

"Let me embrace thee, hug thee; thou have revived my comforts.

"Even if my cousin-King James IV may fail us, our cause will never fail."

John a-Water the politician, Heron the dealer in textile fabrics, Astley the legal clerk, and Skelton the tailor entered the scene.

"Welcome, my tested friends!" Perkin Warbeck said. "You keep your brains awake in our defense.

"Frion, with them carefully consider these affairs, in which all of you be wondrously secret. I will listen to and for what else concerns us here. Be quick and wary."

He exited.

Astley the legal clerk said, "Ah, sweet young prince!"

"Secretary Frion, my fellow-counselors and I have consulted, and we all agree in one opinion precisely: If these Scotch garboils, aka tumults, do not fadge, aka come off as we wish, we will pell-mell and in disorder run among the Cornish choughs immediately and in a trice.

A chough is 1) a chattering bird, or 2) a rustic.

"In a trice" means "without delay."

Skelton the tailor said, "It is but going to sea and leaping ashore in order to cut ten or twelve thousand unnecessary throats, set fire to seven or eight towns, take half a dozen cities, get into the marketplace, crown Perkin Warbeck King Richard IV, and the business is finished."

John a-Water the politician said, "I grant you, say I, so far forth as men may do, no more than men may do; for it is good to consider when consideration may be to the purpose, otherwise — still you shall pardon me — little said is soon amended."

Frion asked, "Then you conclude that the Cornish action is surest?"

Heron the dealer in textile fabrics said, "We do so, and we don't doubt that we shall thrive abundantly. Ho, my masters, had we known of the commotion — the Cornish rebellion — when we set sail out of Ireland, the land had been ours before this time."

Skelton the tailor said, "Bah! Bah! It is but forbearing being an Earl or a Duke a month or two longer. I say, and I say it again, if the work does not go on apace, let me never see new fashion more. I warrant you, I warrant you; we will have it so, and so it shall be."

Astley the legal clerk said, "This is just a cold phlegmatic country, not stirring enough for men of spirit. Give me the heart of England for my money!"

Skelton the tailor said, "A man may batten and grow fat in England in only a week, with hot loaves and butter, and a lusty cup of muscatel wine and sugar at breakfast, though he make never a meal all the month after."

John a-Water the politician said, "Surely, when I bore office I found by experience that to be much troublesome was to be much wise and busy. I have observed how filching, aka stealing, and bragging have been the best service in these last wars; and therefore conclude peremptorily on the design in England. If things and things may fall out, as who can tell what or how — only the end will show it."

Frion said, "Resolved like men of judgment! To linger here a longer time is only to lose time. Cheer the prince, Perkin Warbeck, and hasten him on to this; on this depends fame in success, or glory in our ends."

— 4.3 —

King James IV of Scotland, the Bishop of Durham, and Pedro Hialas talked together. The Bishop of Durham and Pedro Hialas were trying to convince King James IV of Scotland to abandon his support of Perkin Warbeck.

Pedro Hialas said, "France, Spain, and Germany combine a league of amity with England: nothing is lacking for settling peace throughout Christendom, except love between the British monarchs: King James IV of Scotland and King Henry VII of England."

The Bishop of Durham said, "The English merchants, sir, have been received with general procession into Antwerp. The Emperor confirms the alliance."

Formerly, King Henry VII had banned all commercial activity with the Flemish because the Emperor supported Margaret of Burgundy, who supported Perkin Warbeck, but now he was making alliances, including joining the Holy League. Members of the Holy League included the Pope, King Ferdinand II of Aragon, the Holy Roman Emperor, and the rulers of Milan and of Venice. Commercial activity with the Flemish had been resumed.

Pedro Hialas said, "King Ferdinand of Spain is determined on a marriage for his daughter Katherine of Aragon with Prince Arthur, the oldest son of King Henry VII."

The Bishop of Durham said, "France courts this early contract."

Pedro Hialas asked King James IV, "What can hinder a quietness in England?"

The Bishop of Durham gave King James IV the answer, "Only your tolerance of such a silly creature, mighty sir, who is in effect only a ghostly sham, a shadow, a mere trifle."

Pedro Hialas said, "To this union the good of both the church and the commonwealth invites you."

The Bishop of Durham said, "In addition to this unity, a mystery of Providence points out a greater blessing for both these nations than our human reason can search into. King Henry VII has a daughter: the Princess Margaret Tudor. I need not urge what honor, what felicity can follow on such affinity between two Christian Kings allied by ties of blood, but I am sure that if you, sir, ratify the peace proposed, I dare both to promote and effect this marriage for the well-being of both the kingdoms."

In fact, in 1503 King James IV of Scotland married King Henry VII of England's daughter Margaret Tudor. In 1603, their great-grandson, King James VI of Scotland, became King James I of England after the death of Queen Elizabeth I of England.

King James IV asked, "Do you dare to advise that, Lord Bishop?"

The Bishop of Durham replied, "Put it to the test, royal James, by sending some noble personage to the English court by way of embassy."

Pedro Hialas said, "Part of the business shall suit my mediation."

He was willing to go to the English court as an ambassador.

King James IV said, "This is well; what Heaven has ordained to be, must be. You two are the ministers, I hope, of blessed fate.

"But herein only I will stand acquitted: No blood of innocents shall buy my peace."

As he would explain, he was unwilling to hand over Perkin Warbeck to them because he had guaranteed him safety and good treatment in his court.

King James IV continued, "Warbeck, as you call him, came to me, commended by the rulers of Christendom. He was a prince, although he was in distress. His fair demeanor, friendly behavior, and unappalled spirit proclaimed him to be not base in blood, however clouded.

"The brute beasts have both rocks and caves to fly to, and men have the altars of the church where they can find sanctuary. He came to us for refuge: Kings come near in nature to the gods in being touched with pity.

"Yet, noble friends, his mixture with our blood, even with our own, shall in no way interrupt a general peace."

Both King James IV of Scotland and Lady Katherine were descended from King James I of Scotland; by marrying Lady Katherine, Perkin Warbeck had mixed blood with King James IV.

King James IV continued, "I will only dismiss him from my protection, throughout my dominions, in safety, but not ever to return."

Pedro Hialas said, "You are a just King."

The Bishop of Durham said, "You are wise, and therein happy."

King James IV said, "Nor will we delay in affairs of weight.

"Lord Bishop, the Earl of Huntley shall go with you to England as ambassador from us. We will throw down our weapons; peace will be on all sides!

"Now repair to our council; we will soon be with you."

"Delay shall question no dispatch," Pedro Hialas said. "Delay shall not put a prompt settlement in jeopardy. May Heaven crown it."

The Bishop of Durham and Pedro Hialas exited.

King James IV of Scotland said, "An alliance with King Ferdinand II of Aragon! A marriage with the English Margaret Tudor! A free release from restitution for the late affronts — we will not have to pay restitution for damages caused by our Scottish raid into England! Cessation from hostility! And all for Warbeck, not delivered, but dismissed! We could not wish for anything better."

Perkin Warbeck would be dismissed from the Scottish court, but not delivered into the hands of his English enemies.

King James IV called, "Dalyell!"

Lord Dalyell entered the room and said, "Here, sir."

"Have the Earl of Huntley and his daughter been sent for?" King James IV asked.

"Sent for and come, my lord."

"Say to the English prince that we want his company."

"He is at hand, sir," Lord Dalyell replied.

Perkin Warbeck, Lady Katherine, Jane, Frion, Heron, Skelton, John a-Water, and Astley entered the room.

King James IV of Scotland began talking:

"Cousin, our bounty, favors, gentleness, our benefits, and the risk of our person, our people's lives, and our land have evidenced how much we have engaged and risked on your behalf.

"How paltry and how dangerous our hopes appear, how fruitless our attempts in war, how windy, or rather smoky, your assurance of partisanship in your favor shows, we might in vain repeat."

Perkin Warbeck's talk about English citizens flocking to his side had been "windy" — just talk. In addition, it had been "smoky" — it had clouded King James IV's judgment.

King James IV of Scotland continued:

"But now obedience to the mother church, a father's care for his country's commonweal and well-being, and the dignity of state direct our wisdom to seal an oath of peace throughout Christendom. We have already sworn to this oath of peace.

"It is you alone who must seek new fortunes in the world and find a harbor elsewhere. As I promised on your arrival, you have met no treatment deserving repentance in your being here — you have been treated well. But yet I must live as master of what is my own. However, what is necessary for you at your departure, I am well content that you be accommodated with, provided that delay does not prove to be my enemy."

"It shall not, most glorious prince," Perkin Warbeck replied. "The fame of my goals and plans soars higher than rumors of my 'ease' and 'sloth' can aim at. I acknowledge all your boundless and singular favors, and I am only wretched in words as well as means to thank you for the grace that flowed so liberally.

"You're firmly lord of two empires: Scotland and Duke Richard's — my — heart. My claim to my inheritance shall sooner fail than my life shall fail to serve you, the best of Kings.

"And — witness King Edward IV's blood in me! — I am more loath to part with such a great example of virtue — you, King James IV — than all other mere respects.

"But, sir, my last suit is that you will not force from me what you have given — this chaste lady, who is resolute and determined to face all extreme circumstances."

"I am your wife," Lady Katherine said. "No human power can or shall divorce my faith from my duty."

Perkin Warbeck said, "The earth is bankrupt of such another treasure. No one is the treasure that my wife, Lady Katherine, is."

King James IV said to Perkin Warbeck, "I gave her away in marriage to you, cousin, and I must avow and affirm the gift. I will add to that gift, moreover, provisions becoming her high birth and her constancy and chastity that are not suspect to suspicion; I will also provide servants to attend you. We will part good friends."

King James IV exited with Lord Dalyell.

Perkin Warbeck said, "The Tudor — Henry — has been cunning in his plots: His Fox of Durham — Richard Fox, Bishop of Durham — would not fail at last. But so what? Our cause and our courage are our own. Be men, my friends, and let our cousin-King see how we follow fate as willingly as malice follows us. You're all resolved for the west parts of England?"

"Cornwall! Cornwall!" everyone cried.

"The inhabitants expect you daily," Frion said.

Perkin Warbeck ordered, "Cheerfully draw all our ships out of the harbor, friends. Our time of stay seems too long; we must prevent intelligence of our movements reaching Henry Tudor. Moving quickly may prevent that, so let's set about it at once."

"A prince! A prince! A prince!" everyone cried.

This was a cry of support.

Heron, Skelton, Astley, and John a-Water exited. Left behind were Perkin Warbeck, Lady Katherine, Jane Douglas, and Frion.

Perkin Warbeck said to his wife, "Dearest, don't admit into thy pure thoughts the least of scruples, which may charge their softness with a burden of distrust. Should I prove to be lacking the noblest courage now, here would be the test and trial: But I am perfectly assured, sweet; I fear no change more than thy being partner in my suffering."

Lady Katherine replied, "My fortunes, sir, have armed me to encounter whatever chance they meet with."

She then said to Jane Douglas, "Jane, it is fitting that thou stay behind, for whither will thou wander?"

"Never until death will I forsake my mistress, nor even then because I will gladly wish to die with you," Jane Douglas replied.

"Alas, good soul!" Lady Katherine said.

"Sir, to your Aunt Margaret of Burgundy I will relate your present undertakings," Stephen Frion said to Perkin Warbeck. "Expect welcome from her on all occasions. You cannot find me idle in your services."

"Go, Frion, go," Perkin Warbeck said. "Wise men know how to soothe Adversity, not serve it. Thou have served too long on expectation; never yet has any nation read of been so besotted in reason as to adore the setting sun.

"Fly to the Archduke Maximilian's court, and say to the Duchess Margaret of Burgundy that her nephew — me — with fair Katherine his wife, are on their expectation to begin the raising of an empire.

"If they fail, the report and reputation of their attempt will yet never fail.

"Farewell, Frion!"

Stephen Frion exited.

Perkin Warbeck said to his wife about Stephen Frion, "This man, Kate, has been true, although now recently I fear he has been too much familiar with the Fox."

Stephen Frion had spent much time talking with Bishop Fox of Durham.

Lord Dalyell returned, accompanied by the Earl of Huntley, Lady Katherine's father.

The Earl of Huntley said to Perkin Warbeck, "I come to take my leave. You need not fear my interest in this former child of mine; she's all yours now, good sir."

He said to Lady Katherine, his daughter, "Oh, poor lost creature, may Heaven guard thee by giving thee much patience! If thou can, forget thy title to old Huntley's family, as much of peace will settle in thy mind as thou can wish to taste but in thy grave. Yet accept my tears, please; they are tokens of Christian love and charity as truly as of parental affection."

"This is the cruelest farewell!" Lady Katherine said.

The Earl of Huntley said to Perkin Warbeck, "Young gentleman, love this model of my griefs; she calls you husband."

Both the Earl of Huntley and Lady Katherine were crying, and so she was modeling — copying — his griefs.

The Earl of Huntley added, "Then be not jealous of a parting kiss — it is a father's, not a lover's, offering."

He then said to his daughter, "Take it — it is my last."

He kissed her and said, "I am too much a child — I cry. Exchange of passionate grief is of little use; acting like this, I should grow too foolish. May Goodness guide thee!"

He exited, and Lady Katherine said, "I am a most miserable daughter!"

She asked Lord Dalyell, "Have you anything to add, sir, to our sorrows?"

"I resolve, fair lady, with your permission, to wait on all your fortunes in my person, if your lord will grant me acceptance," Lord Dalyell replied.

He was offering to accompany and serve Perkin Warbeck and Lady Katherine on their travels.

"We will be bosom friends, most noble Dalyell," Perkin Warbeck said, "for I accept this tender of your love beyond my ability to speak my thanks for it."

He said to his wife, Lady Katherine, "Clear thy drowned eyes, my fairest. Time and industry will show us better days, or end the worst."

— 4.4 —

The Earl of Oxford and Lord Chamberlain Giles Dawbeney talked together in the Palace of Westminster.

"No news from Scotland yet, my lord?" the Earl of Oxford asked.

"Not any but what King Henry VII knows himself," Lord Chamberlain Giles Dawbeney replied. "I thought that our armies were to have marched that way; the King, it seems, has changed his mind."

"Victory attends his battle standard everywhere," the Earl of Oxford said.

"Wise princes, Earl of Oxford, fight not only with military forces," Lord Chamberlain Giles Dawbeney said. "Providence, aka foresight, directs and tutors strength; else war elephants and armored horses might as well prevail as the subtlest stratagems of war. Both cunning and strength are necessary to win battles."

The Earl of Oxford said, "The Scottish King James IV showed more than common bravery in his offer of a combat hand to hand with the Earl of Surrey."

"And he only *showed* it," Lord Chamberlain Giles Dawbeney said. "Northern bloods are gallant being fired, but the cold climate, without good store of fuel, quickly freezes the glowing flames."

"Surrey, upon my life, would not have shrunk a hair's-breadth," the Earl of Oxford said.

"May he or any Englishman who would not have embraced it with a greediness as violent as hunger runs to food forfeit the honor of an English name and nature!" Lord Chamberlain Giles Dawbeney said. "It was a mark of distinction and honor that any worthy spirit would covet, next to immortality, which is above all the joys of life. We all missed shares in that great opportunity."

King Henry VII, in close conversation with Christopher Urswick, entered the room.

"The King!" the Earl of Oxford said. "Look, he comes smiling."

"Oh, then the game runs smoothly on his side — believe it," Lord Chamberlain Giles Dawbeney said. "Cards well shuffled and dealt with cunning bring some gamblers success, but others must rise from the gambling table as losers."

King Henry VII, as usual, had gathered intelligence, which Lord Chamberlain Giles Dawbeney was comparing to dealing cards with cunning. King Henry VII was expecting Perkin Warbeck to invade England.

In fact, after leaving Scotland, Perkin Warbeck and Lady Katherine sailed to Cork, Ireland. They landed on 16 July 1497, and Perkin Warbeck began making plans to land in Cornwall, England, where he expected to meet with support.

"The lure is working?" King Henry VII asked.

"Most prosperously," Christopher Urswick replied.

King Henry VII had wanted to lure King James IV away from supporting Perkin Warbeck; he had been successful in doing that.

Christopher Urswick, of course, knew of this plan, but the Earl of Oxford and Lord Chamberlain Giles Dawbeney did not, and so Lord Chamberlain Giles Dawbeney had been surprised that King Henry VII's armies had not marched to Scotland.

King Henry VII said, "I knew it would not miss. He foolishly fishes who will stop fishing and hurl his bait into the water because the fish at first plays round about the line and dares not bite. Some plots take time to work."

He said to the others present, "Lords, we may reign as your King yet. Giles Dawbeney, Oxford, Urswick, must Perkin wear the crown?"

"He is a slave!" Lord Chamberlain Giles Dawbeney said.

"He is a vagabond!" the Earl of Oxford said.

"He is a glow-worm!" Christopher Urswick said.

King Henry VII said, "Now, if Frion, his politically practiced schemer, wears a tried and tested brain, 'King' Perkin will in royal procession ride through all his large dominions; let us meet him, and 'tender homage' — ha, sirs! Liegemen ought to pay their fealty."

A liegeman pledged to provide support to a superior lord; in turn, the superior lord pledged to protect the liegeman. Fealty was the duty that a liegeman owed to the superior lord.

Of course, King Henry VII was being sarcastic. He would not offer tender homage to Perkin Warbeck.

"I wish the rascal were, with all his rabble, within twenty miles of London!" Lord Chamberlain Giles Dawbeney said.

"Farther off is near enough to lodge him in his home," King Henry VII said.

They were using metaphors related to animals. A "rascal" is an inferior deer. To "lodge" a buck meant to discover the buck's lodge, aka sleeping place.

King Henry VII added, "I'll wager odds that the Earl of Surrey and all his men are either idle or hastening back here; they don't have work, I suspect, to keep them busy."

King Henry VII had intelligence that peace had been made with King James IV of Scotland, and so the Earl of Surrey was not fighting. Most of the lords present were unaware of this.

"It is a strange idea, sir," Lord Chamberlain Giles Dawbeney said.

Lacking information, he was confused about why King Henry VII would say that.

King Henry VII began to talk about his kingship. He collected taxes but did not waste them. They were spent on such things as intelligence and armies to keep England and his throne safe. He had been merciful — for example, he had pardoned many Cornish rebels — but those to whom he had been merciful were not appreciative and loyal.

He said, "Such voluntary favors" — this was his phrase for tax revenues — "as our people in duty aid us with, we never scattered on cobweb parasites — insubstantial flattering parasites — or lavished out in riotous living or a needless hospitality.

"No undeserving favorite boasts that his income issues from our treasury; our expenses flow through all Europe, proving us to be only the steward of every contribution which provides against the creeping canker of disturbance.

"Is it not striking, then, in this toil of state wherein we are embarked, with breach of sleep, worries and concerns, and the noise of trouble, that our mercy returns neither thanks nor comfort?

"People in the west — Cornwall — still murmur and threaten rebellion, whisper that our government is tyrannical, deny us the tax revenues that are ours, indeed, spurn their lives, of which they are but owners by our gift.

"It must not be."

"It must not and should not be," the Earl of Oxford said.

King Henry VII began, "So then —"

A messenger carrying a packet of letters entered the room.

King Henry VII asked, "To whom are you carrying this packet?"

"This packet is for your sacred majesty," the messenger said, handing the King the packet of letters.

"Sirrah, wait outside," King Henry VII said.

The messenger exited.

"This is news from the North, upon my life," the Earl of Oxford said.

"Wise King Henry VII divines events beforehand; with him attempts and executions are one act," Lord Chamberlain Giles Dawbeney said.

"Urswick, lend me thine ear," King Henry VII said. "Frion has been caught. The man of cunning is outwitted, and we're bound to be safe. Should the reverend John Morton, our aged Archbishop of Canterbury, move to a translation higher yet — if he should become Pope, or die — I tell thee that my Bishop of Durham owns a brain that deserves that see."

A "see" is the area where a Bishop or an Archbishop has ecclesiastical jurisdiction. "Translation" is the movement of a person from one place to another.

He continued, "He's nimble in his industry, and ambitious — do thou hear me?"

"I hear you, and I understand your highness fitly," Christopher Urswick, the King's chaplain, answered.

"Giles Dawbeney and Oxford, since our army stands fully intact, it would be a weakness to permit the rust of laziness to eat among them," King Henry VII said. "Set forward toward Salisbury; the plains are most commodious for their exercise. Ourself will take a muster and conduct a review of them there and/or disband them with reward or else dispose of them as we think best."

"Salisbury!" Lord Chamberlain Giles Dawbeney said. "Sir, all is at peace at Salisbury."

"Dear friend, the responsibility must be our own," King Henry VII said. "We would a little partake in the pleasure of our subjects' ease."

The packet contained letters that informed King Henry VII that Perkin Warbeck was landing at Cornwall. Salisbury was midway between the cities of London and Exeter. After landing in Cornwall, Perkin Warbeck and his supporters would head to Exeter.

"Shall I entreat your loves?" King Henry VII asked.

"Command our lives," the Earl of Oxford replied.

"You are men who know how to take action, not how to forethink and make plans," King Henry VII said. "My Bishop of Durham is a jewel tried and perfect — a jewel, lords. The messenger who brought these letters must speed another letter to the Mayor of Exeter.

"Urswick, do not dismiss the messenger."

"He waits at your pleasure," Christopher Urswick replied.

"Perkin a King?" King Henry VII said. "A King!"

"My gracious lord —" Christopher Urswick began.

King Henry VII interrupted, "Thoughts busied in the sphere of royalty fix not on creeping worms without their stings — these worms are mere dregs of earth. The good use of time results in thriving safety and a wise anticipation of expected ills. We're resolved to go to Salisbury."

— 4.5 —

In September 1497, Perkin Warbeck, Lord Dalyell, Lady Katherine, and Jane Douglas landed on the coast of Cornwall. In the distance, many Cornish citizens shouted in support of them.

Perkin Warbeck said, "After so many storms as wind and seas have threatened our weather-beaten ships, at last, sweet fairest, we have safely arrived on our dear mother earth, ungrateful only to Heaven and us in yielding sustenance to sly usurpers of our throne and right. These general acclamations are an omen of happy progress to their welcome lord. They flock in troops, and with wings of duty fly from all parts to lay their hearts before us."

He then said to his wife, "Unequalled model of a matchless wife, how fares my dearest yet?"

Lady Katherine replied, "I am confirmed in good health, by which I may the better undergo the roughest face of change; but since silence courts affliction, I shall learn the patience to hope. I shall then administer comfort to this truly noble gentleman, Lord Dalyell — a rare unmatched model of a friend! — and to my beloved Jane, the willing follower of all misfortunes."

In addition to their abstract meanings, "silence" referred to Lord Dalyell and Jane Douglas, while "affliction" referred to the afflicted Lady Katherine. Lord Dalyell and Jane Douglas uncomplainingly waited on Lady Katherine, who suffered. By learning how to better bear her suffering, Lady Katherine would comfort Lord Dalyell and Jane Douglas.

Both Lord Dalyell and Jane Douglas denied any special virtue.

Lord Dalyell said, "Lady, I yield only barren crops of premature avowals that are frost-bitten in the spring of fruitless hopes."

Jane Douglas said, "I serve only as the shadow to the body. Madam, without you, let me be nothing."

"Let no one talk of sadness," Perkin Warbeck said. "We are on the way that leads to victory. Let cowards' thoughts dwell with desperate sullenness and despairing melancholy! The lion does not faint when locked in a cage, but when it is loose it disdains all force that bars it from its prey — and we are lion-hearted, or else we are no King of beasts."

Again, his followers shouted in support in the distance.

He said, "Listen to how they shout, triumphant in our cause! Bold confidence marches on bravely and cannot quake at danger."

Skelton the tailor entered the scene and said, "God preserve King Richard IV! God preserve thee, King of hearts! The Cornish blades are men of mettle; throughout the Cornish town of Bodmin and the whole county they have proclaimed my sweet prince to be the Monarch of England. Four thousand brave yeomen — respectable foot-soldiers — with bow and sword already vow to live and die at the foot of King Richard IV."

Astley the legal clerk arrived and said, "The mayor, our fellow counselor, is servant for an emperor. The city of Exeter is appointed for the rendezvous, and nothing lacks for victory but courage and resolution. *Sigillatum et datum decimo Septembris, anno regni regis primo, et cetera, confirmatum est.* All's cocksure and absolutely certain."

The Latin means, "Sealed and dated the tenth of September, in the first year of the reign of our King, etc., it is confirmed."

The King was Perkin Warbeck, aka King Richard IV.

"To Exeter!" Perkin Warbeck ordered. "To Exeter, march on! Commend us to our people. We in person will lend them double spirits; tell them so."

Skelton the tailor and Astley the legal clerk said, "King Richard IV! King Richard IV!"

They exited.

"A thousand blessings guard our lawful arms!" Perkin Warbeck said. "A thousand horrors pierce our enemies' souls! Pale fear unedges their weapons' sharpest points! And when they draw their arrows to the head, numbness shall strike their muscles!

"Such advantage has Majesty in its pursuit of justice that in respect of the proppers-up of Truth's old throne it both enlightens counsel and gives heart to action, while the throats of traitors lie bare before our mercy.

"Oh, divinity of royal birth!"

In this culture, true Kings were believed to get their authority to rule from God.

He continued, "How the divinity of royal birth strikes dumb the tongues whose prodigality of breath is bribed by the partisans to greatness!"

These partisans are bribed to support those who have the crown but are not worthy of it. To Perkin Warbeck, who may have believed that he really was the Duke of York, one such person was King Henry VII.

He continued, "Princes are only men distinguished because of the fineness of their mortal condition, yet they are not so gross and common in beauty of the mind, for there's a fire more sacred that purifies the impure that is in a mixture of pure and impure."

According to Perkin Warbeck, Kings are fine in their mortal condition, and they are fine in the beauty of their mind, for their divine right to rule purifies even their impurities.

He finished, "Herein stand the differences between subjects and Kings: Subjects are men on earth, while Kings are both men and gods."

CHAPTER 5

— 5.1 —

At St. Michael's Mount, a small tidal island off the shore of Cornwall, Lady Katherine and Jane Douglas, wearing riding suits, talked together. One servant was with them. Perkin Warbeck was away with his army, seeking to win the throne of England.

Lady Katherine said, "It is decreed, and we must yield to fate, whose angry justice, although it threatens ruin, contempt, and poverty, is all just a trial of a weak woman's fortitude in suffering. Here, in a foreigner's and an enemy's land" — Lady Katherine was from Scotland and so England was foreign to her — "forsaken and unfurnished of all hopes except such as wait on misery, I wander around, to meet affliction wherever I tread. My retinue and pomp of servants is reduced to one kind gentlewoman and this servant.

"Sweet Jane, to where must we go now?"

"To your ships, dear lady, and turn home," Jane Douglas answered.

"Home!" Lady Katherine said. "I have none. Fly thou to Scotland; thou have friends who will weep for joy to bid thee welcome, but oh, Jane, my Jane! My friends are without hope of comfort, as I must be without hope of them: The common charity — good people's alms and the prayers of the kind-hearted — is the revenue that must support my state.

"As for my native country, since it once saw me a princess in the height of greatness my birth allowed me, here I make a vow that Scotland shall never see me after I have fallen or lessened in my fortunes. Never, Jane, never to Scotland will I return anymore.

"If I could be England's Queen — a glory, Jane, I never aspired to — yet King James IV who gave me away in marriage has sent me with my husband away from his presence, delivered us suspected to his — my husband's — nation, rendered us spectacles to time and pity. And is it fitting that I should return to such as only eagerly listen for our descent from enjoyed happiness to misery that they expect although it is uncertain? Never, never!

"Alas, why do thou weep? And why does that poor creature — my one male servant — wipe his wet cheeks, too? Let me alone feel hardships, I who know to give them harbor. Neither thou nor he has cause to cry: You may live safely."

"There is no safety while your dangers, madam, are in every way apparent," Jane Douglas said.

"Pardon me, lady," the male servant said. "I cannot choose but show my honest heart. You were always my good lady."

"Oh, dear souls," Lady Katherine said. "Your shares in grief are too, too much!"

Lord Dalyell entered the scene and said, "I bring you, fair princess, news of further sadness, more than your sweet youth has been acquainted with yet."

"It is not more, my lord, than I can welcome," Lady Katherine replied. "Speak it. I expect the worst — the worst!"

"All our Cornish allies attacked the city of Exeter, but they were there repulsed by the citizens, who had the help of the Earl of Devonshire and other worthy gentlemen of the country. Your husband then marched to Taunton, and he was there confronted by King Henry VII's Lord Chamberlain Giles Dawbeney.

"King Henry VII himself in person with his army was advancing nearer to renew the fight at the first and every opportunity, but the night before the armies were to join, your husband privately, accompanied with some few horsemen, departed from out the camp, and rode rapidly no one knows to where."

"Fled without battle being first given?" Lady Katherine asked.

"Fled, but followed by Lord Chamberlain Giles Dawbeney," Lord Dalyell replied. "All his supporters were left to taste King Henry VII's mercy — for to that they surrendered — King Henry VII was victorious without bloodshed."

"Oh, my sorrows!" Lady Katherine said. "If both our lives had proved to be the sacrifice to Henry's tyranny, we would have fallen like princes, and robbed him of the glory of his pride."

"Impute your husband's flight not to faintness or to weakness of noble courage, lady, but to foresight," Lord Dalyell said, "for by some secret friend he had intelligence of being bought and sold — betrayed — by his base followers. Worse yet remains untold."

"No, no, it cannot," Lady Katherine said.

"I fear you are betrayed," Lord Dalyell said. "The Earl of Oxford runs hot in pursuit of you."

"He shall not need to," Lady Katherine said. "We'll run as hot in resolution gladly to make the Earl of Oxford our jailor."

"Madam! Madam!" Jane Douglas said. "They come! They come!"

The Earl of Oxford and his soldiers entered the scene.

Drawing his sword, Lord Dalyell said, "Keep back! Or he who dares to rudely and discourteously violate the law of honor runs on my sword."

"Most noble sir, don't," Lady Katherine said to Lord Dalyell.

She then asked the Earl of Oxford, "What reason draws you here, gentlemen? Whom do you seek?"

"Everyone, stand back!" the Earl of Oxford ordered his soldiers.

He then said to Lady Katherine, "With goodwill, lady, from Henry VII, England's King, I would present to the beauteous princess Lady Katherine Gordon the offer of gracious treatment."

"We are that princess whom your master-King pursues with far-reaching arms to draw into his power," Lady Katherine said. "Let him use his tyranny. We shall not be his subject."

"My commission extends no further, most excellent lady, than to the offer of service," the Earl of Oxford said. "It is King Henry VII's pleasure that you, and all who are in your service, be guarded as becomes your birth and greatness. Rest assured, sweet princess, that nothing of what you call yours shall find disturbance, or any welcome other than what suits your high status and rank."

"By what title, sir, may I acknowledge you?" Lady Katherine asked.

"Your servant, lady, descended from the line of Oxford's earls, inherits what his ancestors before him were owners of. I am the Earl of Oxford."

"Your King is herein royal in that he, by a peer so ancient in merit and deserving as well as in blood, commands us to his presence," Lady Katherine said.

"He invites you into his presence, princess," the Earl of Oxford said. "He does not command you."

"Please use your own phrase as you wish," Lady Katherine said. "Both I and mine submit into your protection."

"There's in your number a nobleman whom public reports have spoken well of," the Earl of Oxford said. "The King my master commanded me to say to him how willingly he courts his friendship; this is far from an enforcement, for it is more than what in terms of courtesy so great a prince may hope for."

Lord Dalyell said, "My name is Dalyell."

"It is a name that has won both thanks and wonder from report, my lord," the Earl of Oxford said. "The court of England emulates your merit and covets to embrace you."

"I must wait on the princess — Lady Katherine — in her fortunes," Lord Dalyell replied.

"Will you please, great lady, to set forward?" Lord Dalyell asked Lady Katherine.

"Because I am driven by fate, it would be in vain to strive with Heaven," Lady Katherine said.

They exited.

— 5.2 —

King Henry VII, the Earl of Surrey, and Christopher Urswick talked together at Salisbury. A guard of soldiers was present.

"The counterfeit, King Perkin, has escaped — escaped!" King Henry VII said. "So let him. He is surrounded too fast within the compass of our English domain to steal out of our ports or leap the walls that guard our land; the seas are rough and wider than his weak arms can tug with.

"Surrey, henceforth your King may reign in quiet; turmoils past, like some unquiet dream, have rather busied our imagination than frightened the peace of England. But, Surrey, in negotiating a peace with King James IV of Scotland, why wasn't restitution of the losses that our subjects sustained by the Scotch raids inquired about?"

"Restitution was both demanded and urged, my lord," the Earl of Surrey said, "to which King James IV replied, in modest merriment, but smiling earnestly, that our master Henry VII was much abler to bear the damages than he to repay them."

"The young man, I believe, spoke the honest truth," King Henry VII said. "He endeavors to be wise early in life.

"Urswick, have Sir Rice ap Thomas and Lord Brook our steward given the Western gentlemen who fought against Perkin Warbeck full thanks from us for their proven loyalties?"

"They have," Christopher Urswick said. "The full thanks, as if health and life had reigned among them, they joyfully received with open hearts."

"The young Duke of Buckingham is a fair-natured prince, of great promise, and worthy of his father, who rebelled against and was executed by King Richard III," King Henry VII said. "Attended by a hundred knights and squires of distinguished name, the young Duke of Buckingham tendered humble service, which we must never forget, and the Earl of Devonshire's wounds, although slight, shall find sound cure and appropriate reward in our esteem and favor."

Lord Chamberlain Giles Dawbeney, accompanied by some guards, led into the room Perkin Warbeck, Heron, John a-Water, Astley, and Skelton, all of them chained.

"Life to the King, and safety make secure his throne!" Lord Chamberlain Giles Dawbeney said. "I here present to you, royal sir, a shadow of majesty, but in effect a substance of pity: a young man, grown to ripeness in nothing except the desire for your mercy: Perkin Warbeck, the Christian world's strange wonder."

"Giles Dawbeney, we observe no wonder," King Henry VII replied. "I behold, it is true, an ornament of nature, fine and polished, a handsome youth indeed, but I do not wonder at him. How came he into thy hands?"

"From sanctuary at Beaulieu, near Southampton," Lord Chamberlain Giles Dawbeney said. "There he had registered, with these few followers, as privileged persons."

Perkin Warbeck and these followers had taken sanctuary in an abbey that had granted them sanctuary: As long as they stayed there, they could not be arrested.

Worried that his Lord Chamberlain might have violated the protocol of sanctuary by arresting Perkin Warbeck and these few followers of his, King Henry VII said, "I must not thank you, sir; you would be to blame if you infringed the liberty of sacred houses. Dare we be irreligious?"

"Gracious lord, they voluntarily resigned themselves without compulsion," Lord Chamberlain Giles Dawbeney said.

"They did?" King Henry VII said. "It was done very well; it was done very, very well."

He then said to Perkin Warbeck, "Turn now thine eyes, young man, upon thyself and thy past actions. What revels in violent commotion and tumult through our kingdom a frenzy of aspiring youth has danced, until, lacking breath, thy feet of pride have slipped to break thy neck!"

"But not my heart," Perkin Warbeck replied. "My heart will mount until every drop of blood is frozen by death's perpetual winter. If the sun of majesty should be darkened, let the sun of life be hidden from me in an eclipse that is lasting and universal.

"Sir, remember there was a shooting-in of light when Richmond, not aiming at a crown, retired, and gladly, for comfort to the Duke of Bretaine's court. Richard, who swayed the scepter, was reputed to be a tyrant then. Yet then a dawning glimmered to some few wandering remnants — a dawning promising day when first they ventured on a terrifying shore at Milford Haven."

Perkin Warbeck was referring to King Henry VII's past history. Henry VII had been the Earl of Richmond before becoming King of England. In 1483, he had visited the court of the Duke of Bretaine, aka Brittany. He landed at Milford Haven in Wales and then proceeded to Bosworth Field, where on 22 August 1485 he defeated King Richard III in battle.

"Whither speeds his boldness?" Lord Chamberlain Giles Dawbeney said. "Check his rude tongue, great sir."

"Oh, let him range in his conversation and talk as he pleases," King Henry VII said. "The player's on the stage still: It is his part; he is only acting his part."

He then asked Perkin Warbeck, "What followed?"

"Bosworth Field," Perkin Warbeck said. "There, at an instant, to the world's amazement, a morning to Richmond, and a night to Richard, appeared at one and the same time.

"The tale is soon recognized as similar to my situation.

"Fate, which crowned these attempts when least assured, might have befriended others such as myself who were like you in their resolve to be King."

"A pretty gallant!" King Henry VII said. "Thus your aunt of Burgundy, your duchess-aunt, informed her nephew. And so, the lesson prompted and well memorized, was molded into familiar, easily understood dialogue, often rehearsed, until, learned by heart, it is now received for truth."

"Truth, in her pure simplicity, lacks the skill to put a feigned blush on," Perkin Warbeck replied. "Scorn wears only such fashion as directs attention to gazers' eyes sad, irritated, ulcerated novelty, far beneath the sphere of majesty.

In such a court wisdom and gravity are proper robes by which the sovereign is best distinguished from buffoonish mimics of his greatness."

"Sirrah, change your grotesque pageantry, and now appear in your own nature, or you'll taste the danger of fooling that is out of season and inappropriate," King Henry VII said.

King Henry VII was telling Perkin Warbeck to act like the non-royal man he really was and to stop pretending to be the Duke of York and King Richard IV.

"I expect no less than what severity calls justice, and politicians call safety," Perkin Warbeck said. "Let people who feed on alms beg, but if there can be mercy in a publicly asserted enemy, then may it descend to these poor creatures, my followers, whose involvement with me, for the purpose of the bettering of their fortunes, has instead incurred a loss of all they had. They hoped to better their fortunes by following me, but they have lost everything instead.

"If any charity should flow from some noble orator to them, in death I owe him the fee of thankfulness. I will be grateful from my grave if someone here will speak on their behalf."

"So brave!" King Henry VII said. "What a bold knave is this!"

He then asked, "Which of these rebels has been the Mayor of Cork?"

Lord Chamberlain Giles Dawbeney said sarcastically as he pointed to John a-Water, "This wise formality."

The sarcasm showed that "wise formality" should be better understood as "pompous fool."

Lord Chamberlain Giles Dawbeney ordered, "Kneel to the King, you rascals!"

Perkin Warbeck's supporters knelt.

Perkin Warbeck did not kneel.

"Can thou hope to receive pardon, where thy guilt is so apparent?" King Henry VII asked.

John a-Water replied, "Under your good favors, as men are men, they may err; for I confess, respectively, in taking great sides, the one side prevailing, the other must go down. Herein the point is clear, if the proverb holds, that by destiny, that it is to little purpose to say, this thing or that shall for, as the Fates will have it, so it must be, and who can help it?"

In using "respectively," John a-Water made a blunder. The word he meant was "respectfully."

"Oh, blockhead!" Lord Chamberlain Giles Dawbeney said to John a-Water. "Thou a privy-counselor?"

John a-Water had been one of Perkin Warbeck's privy-counselors.

Lord Chamberlain Giles Dawbeney added, "Beg for your life, and cry aloud, 'Heaven save King Henry!'"

John a-Water said, "Every man knows what is best, as it happens; for my own part, I believe it is true, if I am not deceived, that Kings must be Kings and subjects must be subjects; but which is which, you shall pardon me for that. Whether we speak or hold our peace, all are mortal; no man knows his end."

"We waste time with follies," King Henry VII said.

Heron, John a-Water, Astley, and Skelton all begged, "Mercy, mercy!"

Perkin Warbeck did not join in the cries begging for mercy.

King Henry VII ordered, "Urswick, deliver the dukeling and these fellows to Sir John Digby, the lieutenant of the Tower of London. With safety let them be conveyed to London. It is our pleasure that no uncivil outrage, taunts, or abuse be suffered by their persons: They shall meet fairer law than they deserve. Time may restore their wits, which vain ambition has for many years caused to become unstable."

Perkin Warbeck's followers stood up.

Using the royal plural, Perkin Warbeck said, "Noble thoughts meet freedom in captivity: the Tower of London — our childhood's dreadful nursery!"

"Speak no more!" King Henry VII ordered.

"Come, come," Christopher Urswick ordered Perkin Warbeck and his followers. "You shall have leisure enough to think with."

Christopher Urswick exited with Perkin Warbeck and his followers, who were in the custody of guards.

"Was there ever so much impudence in fraudulent imitation?" King Henry VII said. "The custom, surely, of being called a King has so fastened in his thought that he thinks he really is a King. But we shall teach the lad another language. It is good we have him fast."

Lord Chamberlain Giles Dawbeney said, "The hangman's medicine w
 this saucy humor."

Doctors in this culture believed that the human body had four humors, or vital fluids. Each humor made a contribution to the personality, and for a human being to be sane and healthy, the four humors had to be present in the right amounts. If a man had too much of a certain humor, it would harm his personality and health.

"Very likely," King Henry VII said, "yet we could temper — mix — mercy with extreme severity, if we were not too far provoked."

Normally, people would speak of tempering extreme severity with mercy, but King Henry VII was too far provoked; however, his meaning was clear: He could be merciful — his rule had shown that — if he were not too far provoked and made angry.

The Earl of Oxford, Lady Katherine, Lord Dalyell, Jane Douglas, and some attendants entered the room. Lady Katherine was wearing her richest attire.

"Great sir, be pleased to welcome the Princess Katherine Gordon with your accustomed grace," the Earl of Oxford said.

"Oxford, herein we must censure thy knowledge of our nature," King Henry VII said. "A lady of her birth and virtues could not have found us so unfurnished of good manners as not, on notice given, to have met her halfway in point of love. We need no reminder to treat her well."

He then said to Lady Katherine, "Excuse, fair cousin, the oversight."

She began to kneel, but he said, "Oh, please! You must not kneel; it is most unfitting. First, permit this welcome, a welcome to your own; for you shall find us only the guardian to your fortune and your honors."

"My fortunes and my honors are weak champions, as both are now befriended, sir; however, both bow before your clemency," Lady Katherine said.

"Our arms shall encircle them and protect them from malice," King Henry VII replied.

King Henry VII spoke of her fortune, while Lady Katherine spoke of her fortunes. King Henry VII may have thought that he had decided what her fortune in life would be, while Lady Katherine may have thought that her future life could contain a choice between more than one fortune.

He added, "A sweet lady! Beauty incomparable! Here lives majesty allied with love."

"Oh, sir, I have a husband," Lady Katherine said.

She did not want to become his mistress, if that was what he was after.

"We'll prove to be your father, husband, friend, and servant," King Henry VII said. "Prove what you wish to grant us."

What could she grant the King? Sex, perhaps. He had said that he would prove to be her "husband," so he may have been wanting her to become his mistress.

King Henry VII ordered, "Lords, take care that a patent is immediately drawn for issuing a thousand pounds from our treasury yearly during our cousin's life."

He was granting Lady Katherine a stipend of one thousand pounds per year for as long as she lived.

He continued, "Our Queen, Elizabeth of York, shall be your chief companion, our own court shall be your home, and our subjects all shall be your servants."

He made no mention of her ever returning to Scotland; in fact, Lady Katherine would spend the rest of her life in England and Wales, dying in 1537.

"But my husband?" Lady Katherine asked.

Ignoring Lady Katherine's question about her husband, King Henry VII said to Lord Dalyell, "By all descriptions, you are noble Dalyell, whose generous loyalty has rendered famous a rare and splendid attentive care of Lady Katherine. We thank you. It is a goodness that gives an additional title to every title boasted from your ancestry, which is in everything most worthy."

"Anything worthier than your praises, right princely sir, I need not glory in," Lord Dalyell said.

"Embrace him, lords," King Henry VII said.

As his lords followed his order, he said to Lady Katherine, "Whoever calls you mistress is lifted and taken into our care. A goodlier beauty my eyes have yet never encountered."

He may have been hinting that she was the unchaste mistress of Lord Dalyell. His claim of lifting and taking into his care whoever called her mistress did not apply to her legal husband, Perkin Warbeck, if by "care," he meant "good care." In this society, "mistress" could mean "wife" as well as "a woman who has a long-standing sexual relationship with a man other than her husband."

Lady Katherine said, "Cruel misery of fate! What remains to hope for?"

"Forward, lords, to London," King Henry VII said.

He then said to Lady Katherine, "Fair lady, before long I shall present you with a glad sight, peace, and Huntley's blessing."

Lady Katherine would see her father, the Earl of Huntley, again. King James IV of Scotland had sent him to England as an ambassador to King Henry VII.

— 5.3 —

The constable, some officers, Perkin Warbeck, Christopher Urswick, and Lambert Simnel (formerly a Pretender, but now one of King Henry VII's falconers) went to a place of public punishment. They were followed by the rabble. Some newly built stocks — a structure with holes in which an offender's head and limbs could be restrained — stood there.

King Henry VII had spared Perkin Warwick's life and had let him live at court, although he was always watched. On 9 June 1498, Perkin Warbeck escaped, but he was quickly caught, sentenced to five hours in public stocks, and then imprisoned in the Tower of London. In 1499, he tried to bribe his jailors into helping him seize the Tower of London. He also brought the Earl of Warwick into his plans. King Henry VII discovered the plot and sentenced both Perkin Warwick and the Earl of Warwick to death.

The constable ordered the rabble, "Make room there! Keep off, I order you, and none of you come within twelve feet of his majesty's new stocks, upon pain of displeasure."

He ordered, "Bring forth the malefactor."

They brought forth Perkin Warbeck, and the constable said to him, "Friend, you must endure this business; there is no avoiding it."

He ordered, "Open the hole, and in with his legs, just in the middle hole; there, that hole."

They put Perkin Warbeck in the stocks. Normally, one hole would restrain one limb or the head, but in this case both of Perkin Warbeck's legs were placed in the hole for the head. The stocks were then closed around his ankles.

The constable ordered the rabble, "Keep off, or I'll imprison you all. Shall not a man in authority be obeyed!"

He then said, "So, so, there; it is as it should be."

He ordered, "Put on the padlock, and give me the key."

The constable ordered the rabble, "Off, I say, keep off!"

Christopher Urswick said, "Even now, Warbeck, clear thy conscience. Thou have tasted King Henry's mercy liberally; the law has forfeited thy life."

He was using the less respectful "thou" and "thy" when talking to Perkin Warbeck, who had been sentenced to death by hanging. This method of execution was used for commoners. Royal prisoners such as the Earl of Warwick were executed by beheading.

Christopher Urswick continued, "A fair, impartial jury has sentenced thee to the gallows."

It was a jury of one: King Henry VII.

He continued, "Twice most wickedly, most desperately, thou have escaped from the Tower of London, inveigling to thy party with thy witchcraft young Edward, Earl of Warwick, son to the Earl of Clarence. The Earl of Warwick's head must pay the price of that attempt, that poor gentleman, unhappy in his fate, and ruined by thy cunning!

"So a mongrel — you, a commoner — may pluck the true stag — the Earl of Warwick, a noble — down. Yet, yet, confess thy parentage; for yet the King has mercy."

Lambert Simnel said, "You would be Dick the Fourth — very likely! Your pedigree has been published; you are known to be Osbeck's son of Tournay, Belgium. You are a loose runagate, a wanderer, and a landloper and land rover, and your father was a Jew who turned Christian merely to repair his miseries. Where's now your kingship?"

"Am I to be tormented to my death?" Perkin Warbeck said. "Intolerable cruelty! I laugh at the Duke of Richmond's intrigue against my fortunes."

He still refused to call Henry VII the King of England.

He continued, "Those in possession of a crown have never lacked heralds."

In other words, anyone who wears a crown will have heralds who declare that the crown-wearer is in fact King, whether or not he biologically deserves to be King.

"You will not know who I am?" Lambert Simnel said. "You refuse to acknowledge who I am?"

Christopher Urswick said to Perkin Warbeck, "He is Lambert Simnel, your predecessor in a dangerous rebellion. But, on his submission to King Henry VII, he was not just received to grace and allowed to live, but by the King he was granted his service. The King gave him a job."

Lambert Simnel said, "I, who would be the Earl of Warwick, toiled and battled against my master, King Henry VII, and I leaped to catch the moon and boasted that my name was Plantagenet, as you do. An earl, indeed! When in truth I was, as you are, a complete and utter rascal. Yet his majesty, a prince composed of sweetness — may Heaven protect him! — forgave me all my villainies, reprieved the sentence of a shameful end, accepted my guarantee of obedience to his service, and I am now his falconer, live plenteously, eat at the King's expense, enjoy the sweetness of liberty and favor, and sleep securely. And is not this, now, better than to struggle against the hangman's clutches, or to encounter the cordage of a tough noose that will break your neck?"

Referring to Perkin Warbeck, he said, "So, then, the gallant totters!"

One meaning of "totters" is "hangs and swings from the gallows." Another meaning is "wavers," as in this case "thinks about taking back his claim to be the rightful King of England."

Switching to the less respectful "thee," Lambert Simnel said, "Please, Perkin, let my example lead thee; be no longer a counterfeit; confess, and hope for pardon."

"For pardon!" Perkin Warbeck said, scornfully. "Hold, my heartstrings, while contempt of calumnies, in scorn, may bid defiance to this base man's foul language!

"Thou poor vermin, how dare thou creep so near me? Thou an earl! Why, thou enjoy as much of happiness as all the driving power of slight ambition flew at. A dunghill was thy cradle. So a puddle, by virtue of the sunbeams, breathes forth a dangerous vapor to infect the purer air, which drops again into the muddy womb that first exhaled it. Bread and a slavish ease, with some protection from the base beadle's whip, crowned all thy hopes.

"But, sirrah, if there ran in thy veins one drop of such a royal blood as flows in mine, thou would not change thine condition to be second in England's state, without the crown itself. Coarse creatures are incapable of excellence.

"But let the world, as all to whom I am this day a spectacle, to time deliver, and by tradition pass on to posterity without any other chronicle than truth, how steadfastly my resolution suffered a martyrdom of majesty."

"He's past recovery," Lambert Simnel said. "A Bedlam cannot cure him."

Bedlam was London's Bethlem Royal Hospital; it served the mentally ill.

Christopher Urswick ordered, "Leave. Inform the King about his behavior."

Lambert Simnel said, "Perkin, beware the rope! The hangman's coming."

He exited to carry out his orders.

Christopher Urswick said to Perkin Warbeck, "If yet thou have no pity for thy body, pity thy soul!"

This society believed in confessing sins, including lies, before death in order to escape eternal damnation.

Lady Katherine, Jane Douglas, Lord Dalyell, and the Earl of Oxford entered the scene.

Jane Douglas said, "Dear lady!"

The Earl of Oxford said to Lady Katherine, "Where are you, careless of shame, going?"

He felt that Lady Katherine ought to be ashamed of herself for visiting the criminal Perkin Warbeck, although Perkin Warbeck was her husband.

"Have patience with me, sir," Lady Katherine replied, "and don't trouble and disturb the current of my duty. Leave me alone."

She said to her husband, "Oh, my loved lord! Can any scorn be yours in which I have no interest?"

Wanting to join him in the stocks, she said, "Some kind hand, lend me assistance, so that I may partake in and have a share of the infliction of this penance."

She then said to her husband, "My life's dearest, forgive me. I have stayed too long from tendering attendance on your disgrace; yet bid me welcome."

"Great miracle of loyalty!" Perkin Warbeck said. "My miseries were never bankrupt of their confidence in even the worst afflictions, until this time; now I feel the worst afflictions."

Because his wife was sharing in his miseries, he now truly felt them. He loved his wife and did not want her to feel miserable.

He continued, "Reputation and thy own merits, thou best of creatures, might to eternity have stood as an example for every virtuous wife without this conquest — this moral victory. Thou have outdone belief; yet may their ruin in marriages-to-come be never pitied, to whom thy story shall appear an unbelievable fable!

"Why would thou prove to be so much unkind to your greatness of rank as to glorify thy vows by such a servitude of loyalty to me, your husband? I cannot weep, but trust me, dear, my heart is filled with strong emotion."

In an apostrophe, he addressed King Henry VII, who was not present: "Harry Richmond, a woman's faith has robbed thy fame of triumph."

The Earl of Oxford said, "Sirrah, stop your deceiving, and tie up the devil that ranges in your tongue."

Christopher Urswick said, "Thus witches, possessed and deluded even to their deaths, say that they have been wolves and dogs, and sailed in eggshells over the sea, and rode on fiery dragons and travelled in the air more than a thousand miles, all in a night.

"Satan, the enemy of mankind, is powerful, but false, and falsehood is confident."

"Remember, lady, who you are," the Earl of Oxford said. "Come away from that impudent impostor."

Lady Katherine was a noble, the Earl of Oxford was saying, while Perkin Warbeck was a commoner who was pretending to be a noble.

"You abuse us," Lady Katherine replied. "For when the holy churchman joined our hands, our vows were real then; the ceremony was not an illusion, but an actuality."

She said to Perkin Warbeck, "Whatever these people call thee, I am certain that thou are my husband. No divorce in Heaven has been filed in court between us; it is an injustice for any earthly power to divide us. Either we will live together, or let us die together. There is a cruel mercy."

Perkin Warbeck said, "Despite the tyranny of Henry, we reign in our affections, blessed woman! Read in my destiny the wreck of honor. Point out, in my contempt of death, to the memory of posterity some miserable happiness; since herein, even when I fell, I stood enthroned a monarch of one chaste wife's pure and uncorrupted loyalty in marriage. Fair angel of perfection, immortality shall raise thy name up to an adoration, immortality shall court every high opinion of true merit for thy name, and immortality shall enroll your name as a saint in the calendar of Virtue, when I am turned into the self-same dust from which I was first formed."

The Earl of Oxford said to Lady Katherine, "The lord ambassador, the Earl of Huntley, your father, madam, should he look on your strange subjection of yourself in talking to this commoner in so public a gaze, would blush on your behalf, and wish he had never left his country of Scotland because such a sight would give him such sorrow."

"Why are thou angry, Oxford?" Lady Katherine said. "I must be more resolute in my duty."

She said to her husband, "Sir, don't impute it to immodesty that I presume to press you to a legacy before we part forever."

The legacy would be something to remember him by.

"Let the legacy be, then, my heart, the rich remains of all my fortunes," Perkin Warbeck said.

"Confirm it with a kiss, please," Lady Katherine said.

"Oh, with that kiss I wish to breathe my last!" Perkin Warbeck said. "Upon thy lips, those equal twins of comeliness, I seal the testament of honorable vows."

He kissed her.

He added, "Whoever be that man who shall unkiss this sacred imprint next, may he prove more prosperous than I in this world's just applause, but not more desertful than I!"

"By this sweet pledge of both our souls, I swear to die a faithful widow to thy bed, not to be forced or won," Lady Katherine said. "Oh, never, never!"

The Earl of Surrey, the Earl of Huntley, the Earl of Crawford, and Lord Chamberlain Giles Dawbeney entered the scene.

Lord Chamberlain Giles Dawbeney ordered, "Free the condemned person from the stocks; quickly free him from them! What has he confessed by now?"

They took Perkin Warbeck out of the stocks.

"Nothing to the purpose," Christopher Urswick said. "Still he will be King. He will not admit that he is actually a commoner."

The Earl of Surrey said to Perkin Warbeck, "Prepare your journey to a new kingdom, then, unhappy, willfully foolish madman!"

He said to Lady Katherine's father, the Earl of Huntley, "See, my lord ambassador, your lady daughter will not leave the counterfeit in this disfavor of fate."

The Earl of Huntley said to his daughter, Lady Katherine, "I never appointed thy marriage to this man, girl, but yet, being married, enjoy thy duty to a husband freely. The griefs are mine. I glory in thy loyalty to your husband, and I must not say that I wished that I had missed some part in these trials of a patience."

"You will forgive me, noble sir?" Lady Katherine asked.

"Yes, yes," her father said. "In every duty of a wife and daughter, I dare not disavow and disown thee.

"To your husband — for such you are, sir — I impart a farewell of manly pity; what your life has passed through, the dangers of your end will make apparent. And I can add, to give comfort to your suffering, no cordial, but the wonder of your person, which keeps so firm a station. You are a mere mortal man, but you are making a firm stand. We are now parted."

"We are," Perkin Warbeck said. "May a crown of peace renew thy age, most honorable Huntley!

"Worthy Crawford! We may embrace; I never thought to give thee injury."

It was customary for a condemned man to make peace as much as possible with those around him, including — immediately before death — the executioner.

"Nor was I ever guilty of neglect that might procure such a thought," the Earl of Crawford said. "I take my leave now, sir."

"To you, Lord Dalyell — what?" Perkin Warbeck said. "Accept a sigh — it is hearty and in earnest."

"I lack utterance; I cannot speak," Lord Dalyell said. "My silence is my farewell."

Near fainting, Lady Katherine cried, "Oh! Oh!"

Supporting her, Jane Douglas said, "Sweet madam, what is this?"

She said to Lord Dalyell, "My lord, your hand."

Lord Dalyell supported Lady Katherine and said, "Dear lady, be pleased that I may attend you to your lodging."

Lord Dalyell and Jane Douglas, both supporting Lady Katherine, exited.

The Sheriff and some officers arrived with Skelton, Astley, Heron, and John a-Water, who had nooses around their necks.

"Look," the Earl of Oxford said to Perkin Warbeck. "Behold your followers, appointed to wait on you in death!"

Perkin Warbeck said to his followers, "Why, peers of England, we'll lead them on courageously. I read a triumph over tyranny upon their individual foreheads.

"Faint not in the moment of victory! Our ends, and Warwick's head, innocent Warwick's head — for we are only the prologue to his tragedy — conclude the wonder of Henry's fears, and then the glorious race of fourteen Kings, all of them Plantagenets, terminates in this last male child. Heaven be obeyed!"

There were fourteen Plantagenet Kings, ranging from King Henry II to King Richard III. The Earl of Warwick — the man whom Lambert Simnel had pretended to be, was the last male descended from the kingly Plantagenet line. With his death, King Henry VII — the first Tudor King — no longer had to fear rebellion from or in support of the Plantagenets.

The deaths of Perkin Warbeck and his followers were the prologue to the Earl of Warbeck's death. On 23 November 1499, an executioner hanged Perkin Warbeck. On 28 November 1499, an executioner beheaded the Earl of Warbeck.

Perkin Warbeck continued, "We will impoverish time of its power to be amazed, friends, and we will prove to be as trusty in our payments as we prove to be prodigal to nature in our debts. We will act finely as we pay the debt — death — we owe to nature.

"Death? Bah! It is only a sound, a name of air — a minute's storm, or not so much.

"To tumble from bed to bed, be mangled and mutilated alive by some physicians, for a month or two, in hope of gaining freedom from a fever's torments, might make a man's courage stagger; but here in execution the pain is already over before it can be acutely felt.

"Be men of spirit! Spurn coward passion! So illustrious mention shall blaze and proclaim our names, and call us Kings over Death."

Lord Chamberlain Giles Dawbeney said, "Away, impostor beyond precedent!"

The Sheriff and officers exited with the prisoners, including Perkin Warbeck.

Lord Chamberlain Giles Dawbeney added, "No chronicle records his fellow."

The Earl of Huntley said, "I have no thoughts left: It is sufficient in such cases that just laws ought to proceed."

King Henry VII, the Bishop of Durham, and Pedro Hialas entered the scene.

King Henry VII said to the Earl of Huntley, "We have made up our mind. Your business, noble lords, shall find such a successful result as your King James IV importunes."

"You are gracious," the Earl of Huntley replied.

King Henry VII said, "Perkin, we are informed, is prepared to die. In that we'll honor him. Our lords shall follow to see the execution; and from hence we gather this fit moral lesson:

"Public governments and kingdoms, like our particular bodies, experience the most good in health when purged of corrupted blood."

EPILOGUE

Here has appeared, although in a diverse and varied fashion,
   The threats of majesty, the strength of passion,
   Hopes of an empire, change of fortunes; all
   The great events that can to the theaters of greatness — kingdoms — fall,
   Proving their weak foundations. Who will please,
   Amongst such several sights, to judge these
   To be no births abortive, nor a bastard brood —
   Shame to a parentage or fosterhood —
   May sanction by their kindness all our just excuses,
   And often find a welcome to the company of the Muses.

NOTES

— 2.3 —

Skelton, a tailor, says this:

For fashioning of shapes and cutting a cross-caper,
turn me off to my trade again. (2.3.170-171)

Source: John Ford, *The Chronicle History of Perkin Warbeck: A Strange Truth*. Ed. Peter Ure. The Revels Plays. London: Methuen & Co, Ltd., 1968.

The word "shapes" has a double meaning: A shape can be 1) an attitude in dancing, or 2) a costume.

We would expect some kind of double meaning in "cross-caper," which is a move in dancing.

"Cross-caper" may be a reference to sitting cross-legged while working as a tailor. This may seem to many people to be an uncomfortable position, but apparently tailors traditionally worked while in that position.

The below information comes from this source:

"A tailor's seat — Is this still the way tailors work?" Ask Andy About Clothes. 23 January 2015 <http://tinyurl.com/y6mbx47v>:

The National Library of Ireland has an interesting old photograph on it's [sic] Flickr page[1], showing tailors hard at work in a long gone establishment called Hearne's, in Waterford.

Taken in 1907, it shows a disguising of tailors, (yes, I looked it up and that is the proper collective noun for tailors[2]), all sitting cross-legged on the floor while they work. Most are sewing, but one man on the right hand side has a small ironing board[3] on his knee.

---

1. https://www.flickr.com/photos/nlireland/16222784641/

2. http://users.tinyonline.co.uk/gswithenbank/collnoun.htm#People

3. http://i.viglink.com/?key=1af6cb019f4ed83a5f49f3a51104f449&insertId=e9ad5717057a4104&type=KW&exp=60%3ACI1C55A%3A15&libId=ju3bjz5s010004nt000DAbyvpm5bw&loc=https%3A%2F%2Faskandyaboutclothes.com%2Fforum%2Fthreads%2Fa-tailors-seat-is-this-still-the-way-tailors-work.200038%2F&v=1&iid=e9ad5717057a4104&opt=true&out=https%3A%2F%2Fwww.amazon.com%2FIroning-Boards-Space-Saving-Irons-Steamers%2Fs%3Fie%3DUTF8%26page%3D1%26rh%3Dn%253A510246%252Cp_n_feature_keywords_browse-

I was initially surprised at this seemingly uncomfortable way to sit while working, but several people commented that this is the traditional way for a tailor to sit. Is this still the case?

This is Andy's answer:

This is actually the traditional way tailors worked, seated on the floor or even on raised platforms and is known as sitting tailor style or tailor fashion[4].

My great grandfather was a tailor in Glasgow and worked sitting like this on a raised platform in front of the window. I've seen the same technique used by modern day tailors in Romania.

The Wikipedia article on "Sartorius muscle" has this information:

Sartorius comes from the Latin[5] word sartor, *meaning tailor, and it is sometimes called the tailor's muscle.*

This name was chosen in reference to the cross-legged position in which tailors once sat. In French, the muscle name itself "couturier" comes from this specific position which is referred to as "sitting as a tailor" (in French: "s'asseoir en tailleur").

There are other hypotheses as to the genesis of the name. One is that it refers to the location of the inferior portion of the muscle being the "inseam" or area of the inner thigh that tailors commonly measure when fitting trousers. Another is that the muscle closely resembles a tailor's ribbon. Additionally, antique sewing

bin%253A2839841011&ref=https%3A%2F%2Fwww.google.com%2F&title=A%20tailor%27s%20seat%20-%20Is%20this%20still%20the%20way%20tailors%20work%3F%20%7C%20Ask%20Andy%20FORUMS&txt=%3Cspan%3Esmall%20%3C%2Fspan%3E%3Cspan%3Eironing%20%3C%2Fspan%3E%3Cspan%3Eboard%3C%2Fspan%3E

4.   *http://i.viglink.com/?key=1af6cb019f4ed83a5f49f3a51104f449&insertId=8f27942dbdc0d20d&type=H&exp=60%3ACII CS5A%3A15&libId=ju3bjz5s010004nt000DAbyvpm5bw&loc=https%3A%2F%2Faskandyaboutclothes.com%2Fforum%2Fthreads%2Fa-tailors-seat-is-this-still-the-way-tailors-work.200038%2F&v=1&iid=8f27942dbdc0d20d&opt=true&out=https%3A%2F%2Frover.ebay.com%2Fro ver%2F1%2F711-53200-19255-0%2F1%3Ftoolid%3D10029%26campid%3DCAMPAIGNID%26customid%3DCUSTOMID%26catId%3D11450%26type%3D2%26ext%3D254160276873%26item%3D254160276873&ref=https%3A%2F%2Fwww.google.com%2F&title=A%20tailor%27s%20seat%20-%20Is%20this%20still%20the%20way%20tailors%20work%3F%20%7C%20Ask%20Andy%20FORUMS&txt=%3Cspan%3Etailor%20%3C%2Fspan%3E%3Cspan%3Efashion%3C%2Fspan%3E*

5.   *https://en.wikipedia.org/wiki/Latin*

machines required continuous cross body pedaling. This combination of lateral rotation and flexion of the hip and flexion of the knee gave tailors particularly enlarged sartorius muscles.

Source of above information: "Sartorius muscle." Wikipedia. Accessed 4 April 2019

<https://en.wikipedia.org/wiki/Sartorius_muscle>.

Note: *The Oxford English Dictionary*'s earliest citation for "sartorius," which it defines as "A long narrow muscle which crosses the thigh obliquely in front" is from 1704.

Finally, this is a reference to Elizabethan tailors sitting cross-legged:

They sit at their meat as tailors sit upon their stalls cross-legged [...].

Source of above information: *A Last Elizabethan Journal, Volume 3.* By G.B. Harrison. Routledge, 1999. Accessed 4 April 2019 <http://tinyurl.com/y5vpr6zy>. The reference is from "Sir Anthony Shirley's Travels," p. 214.

— 3.1 —

Our Cornish rebels, cozened of their hopes,

Met brave resistance by that country's earl,

George Abergeny, Cobham, Poynings, Guilford,

And other loyal hearts (3.1.18-21)

Source: John Ford, *The Chronicle History of Perkin Warbeck: A Strange Truth*. Ed. Peter Ure. The Revels Plays. London: Methuen & Co, Ltd., 1968.

Cornwall's "earl, George Abergeny" is probably George Nevill, 5th Baron Bergavenny.

The below information comes from Wikipedia:

George Nevill, 5th Baron Bergavenny KG[6], PC[7] (c.1469 – 1535), the family name often written Neville, was an English nobleman and courtier who held the office of Lord Warden of the Cinque Ports[8]. [...] As a second cousin of the new Queen, Anne Nevill[9], he attended the coronation of King Richard III[10] in 1483 when, despite his young age, he was knighted. Having succeeded to his father's

---

6.	*https://en.wikipedia.org/wiki/Knight_of_the_Garter*

7.	*https://en.wikipedia.org/wiki/Privy_Council_of_England*

8.	*https://en.wikipedia.org/wiki/Lord_Warden_of_the_Cinque_Ports*

9.	*https://en.wikipedia.org/wiki/Anne_Neville*

10.	*https://en.wikipedia.org/wiki/Richard_III_of_England*

peerage and estates in 1492, he achieved prominence fighting against the Cornish rebels in 1497 at the Battle of Blackheath[11].

Source of Above Information: "George Nevill, 5th Baron Bergavenny." Wikipedia. Accessed 25 April 2019 <https://tinyurl.com/y6ok3xuu>.

The below information comes from Wikipedia:

Earl of Cornwall

The title of Earl of Cornwall was created several times in the Peerage of England[12] before 1337, when it was superseded by the title Duke of Cornwall[13], which became attached to heirs-apparent to the throne.

Source of Above Information: "Earl of Cornwall." Wikipedia. Accessed 25 April 2019. <https://tinyurl.com/y5tvpkkf>.

— 5.3 —

A Constable says this:

Make room there! Keep off, I require ye; and none come
within twelve foot of his majesty's new stocks, upon pain of
displeasure. — Bring forward the malefactors. — Friend,
you must to this gear, no remedy. — Open the hole, and in
with his legs, just in the middle hole; there, that hole.

Source: John Ford, *The Chronicle History of Perkin Warbeck: A Strange Truth*. Ed. Peter Ure. The Revels Plays. London: Methuen & Co, Ltd., 1968.

These are unusual stocks, perhaps, or perhaps the way they are used is unusual: Both feet are placed in the middle hole. I wonder whether both legs are placed in the hole that is meant for a head.

This is possible because these are stocks, not a pillory. A pillory is a set of stocks placed on a post so that the prisoner is standing. Perkin Warbeck must be sitting while his legs are in the stocks.

---

11.   *https://en.wikipedia.org/wiki/Battle_of_Blackheath*

12.   *https://en.wikipedia.org/wiki/Peerage_of_England*

13.   *https://en.wikipedia.org/wiki/Duke_of_Cornwall*

APPENDIX A: BRIEF HISTORICAL BACKGROUND

KING EDWARD III: 1327-1377

Son of King Edward II, he reigned for a long time — 50 years. Because he wanted to conquer Scotland and France, he started the Hundred Years War in 1338. King Edward III and his eldest son, Edward the Black Prince, won important victories against the French in the Battle of Crécy (1346) and the Battle of Poitiers (1356).

One of King Edward III's sons was John of Gaunt, first Duke of Lancaster.

Another of King Edward III's sons was Edmund of Langley, first Duke of York.

During his reign, the Black Death — the bubonic plague — struck in 1348-1350 and killed half of England's population.

KING RICHARD II: 1377-deposed 1399

King Richard II was the son of Edward the Black Prince. In 1381, Wat Tyler led the Peasants Revolt, which was suppressed. King Richard II sent Henry, Duke of Lancaster, into exile and seized Henry's estates, but in 1399 Henry, Duke of Lancaster, returned from exile and deposed King Richard II, thereby becoming King Henry IV. In 1400, King Richard II was murdered in Pontefract Castle, which is also known as Pomfret Castle.

HOUSE OF LANCASTER

KING HENRY IV: 1399-1413

Henry, Duke of Lancaster, was the son of John of Gaunt, who was the third son of King Edward III. He was born at Bolingbroke Castle and so was also known as Henry of Bolingbroke. Returning from exile in France to reclaim his estates, he deposed King Richard II. He spent the 13 years of his reign putting down rebellions and defending himself against those who would assassinate or depose him. The Welshman Owen Glendower and the English Percy family were among those who fought against him. King Henry IV died at the age of 45.

KING HENRY V: 1413-1422

The son of King Henry IV, King Henry V renewed the war with France. He and his army defeated the French at the Battle of Agincourt (1415) despite being heavily outnumbered. He married Catherine of Valoise, the daughter of the French King, but he died before becoming King of France. He left behind a 10-month-old son, who became King Henry VI.

KING HENRY VI: 1422-deposed 1461; briefly returned to the throne in 1470-1471

The Hundred Years War ended in 1453; the English lost all land in France except for Calais, a port city. After King Henry VI suffered an attack of mental illness in 1454, Richard, third Duke of York and the father of King Henry IV and King Richard III, was made Protector of the Realm. England suffered civil war after the House of York challenged King Henry VI's right to be King of England. In 1470, King Henry VI was briefly restored to the English throne. In 1471, he was murdered in the Tower of London. A short time previously, his son, Edward, Prince of Wales, had been killed at the Battle of Tewkesbury in 1471; this was the final battle in the Wars of the Roses. The Yorkists decisively defeated the Lancastrians.

King Henry VI founded both Eton College and King's College, Cambridge.

WARS OF THE ROSES

From 1455-1487, the Yorkists and the Lancastrians fought for power in England in the Wars of the Roses. The emblem of the York family was a white rose, and the emblem of the Lancaster family was a red rose. The Yorkists and the Lancastrians were descended from King Edward III.

HOUSE OF YORK

KING EDWARD IV: 1461-1483 (King Henry VI briefly returned to the throne in 1470-1471)

Son of Richard, third Duke of York, he charged his brother George, Duke of Clarence, with treason and had him murdered in 1478. After dying suddenly, he left behind two sons aged 12 and 9, and five daughters.

His surviving two brothers in Shakespeare's play *Richard III* are these: 1) George, Duke of Clarence. Clarence is the second-oldest brother; and 2) Richard, Duke of Gloucester, and afterwards King Richard III. Gloucester is the youngest surviving brother.

William Caxton established the first printing press in Westminster during King Edward IV's reign.

KING EDWARD V: 1483-1483

The eldest son of King Edward IV, he reigned for only two months, the shortest-lived monarch in English history. He was 13 years old. He and his younger brother, Richard, Duke of York, were murdered in the Tower of London. According to Shakespeare's play, their uncle, Richard, Duke of Gloucester, who became King Richard III, was responsible for their murders.

KING RICHARD III: 1483-1485

Brother of King Edward IV, Richard, the Duke of Gloucester, declared the two Princes in the Tower of London — King Edward V and Richard, Duke of York — illegitimate and made himself King Richard III. In 1485, Henry Tudor, Earl of Richmond, a descendant of John of Gaunt, who was the father of King Henry IV, defeated King Richard III at the Battle of Bosworth Field in Leicestershire. King Richard III died in that battle.

King Richard III's father was Richard Plantagenet, Duke of York. His mother was Cecily Neville, Duchess of York.

King Richard III's death in the Battle of Bosworth Field is regarded as marking the end of the Middle Ages in England.

A NOTE ON THE PLANTAGENETS

The first Plantagenet King was King Henry II (1154-1189). From 1154 until 1485, when King Richard III died, all English Kings were Plantagenets. Both the Lancaster family and the York family were Plantagenets.

Geoffrey Plantagenet, Count of Anjou, was the founder of the House of Plantagenet. Geoffrey's son, Henry Curtmantle, became King Henry II of England, thereby founding the Plantagenet dynasty. Geoffrey wore a sprig of broom, a flowering shrub, as a badge; the Latin name for broom is *planta genista*, and from it the name "Plantagenet" arose.

The Plantagenet dynasty can be divided into three parts:

1154-1216: The Angevins. The Angevin Kings were Henry II, Richard I (Richard the Lionheart), and John 1.

1216-1399: The Plantagenets. These Kings ranged from King Henry III to King Richard II.

1399-1485: The Houses of Lancaster and of York. These Kings ranged from King Henry IV to King Richard III.

BEGINNING OF THE TUDOR DYNASTY

KING HENRY VII: 1485-1509

When King Richard III fell at the Battle of Bosworth, Henry Tudor, Earl of Richmond, became King Henry VII. A Lancastrian, he married Elizabeth of York — young Elizabeth of York in William Shakespeare's *Richard III* — and united the two warring houses, York and Lancaster, thus ending the Wars of the Roses. One of his grandfathers was Sir Owen Tudor, who married Catherine of Valoise, widow of King Henry V. The reign of King Henry VII was troubled by Pretenders to the throne; these Pretenders included Lambert Simnell and Perkin Warbeck.

KING HENRY VIII: 1509-1547

King Henry VIII had six wives. These are their fates: "Divorced, Beheaded, Died, Divorced, Beheaded, Survived." He divorced his first wife, Catherine of Aragon, so that he could marry Anne Boleyn. Because of this, England divorced itself from the Catholic Church, and King Henry VIII became the head of the Church of England. King Henry VIII had one son and two daughters, all of whom became rulers of England: Edward, daughter of Jane Seymour; Mary, daughter of Catherine of Aragon; and Elizabeth, daughter of Anne Boleyn.

APPENDIX B: ABOUT THE AUTHOR

It was a dark and stormy night. Suddenly a cry rang out, and on a hot summer night in 1954, Josephine, wife of Carl Bruce, gave birth to a boy — me. Unfortunately, this young married couple allowed Reuben Saturday, Josephine's brother, to name their first-born. Reuben, aka "The Joker," decided that Bruce was a nice name, so he decided to name me Bruce Bruce. I have gone by my middle name — David — ever since.

Being named Bruce David Bruce hasn't been all bad. Bank tellers remember me very quickly, so I don't often have to show an ID. It can be fun in charades, also. When I was a counselor as a teenager at Camp Echoing Hills in Warsaw, Ohio, a fellow counselor gave the signs for "sounds like" and "two words," then she pointed to a bruise on her leg twice. Bruise Bruise? Oh yeah, Bruce Bruce is the answer!

Uncle Reuben, by the way, gave me a haircut when I was in kindergarten. He cut my hair short and shaved a small bald spot on the back of my head. My mother wouldn't let me go to school until the bald spot grew out again.

Of all my brothers and sisters (six in all), I am the only transplant to Athens, Ohio. I was born in Newark, Ohio, and have lived all around Southeastern Ohio. However, I moved to Athens to go to Ohio University and have never left.

At Ohio U, I never could make up my mind whether to major in English or Philosophy, so I got a bachelor's degree with a double major in both areas, then I added a Master of Arts degree in English and a Master of Arts degree in Philosophy. Yes, I have my MAMA degree.

Currently, and for a long time to come (I eat fruits and veggies), I am spending my retirement writing books such as *Nadia Comaneci: Perfect 10*, *The Funniest People in Dance*, *Homer's* Iliad: *A Retelling in Prose*, and *William Shakespeare's* Othello: *A Retelling in Prose*.

By the way, my sister Brenda Kennedy writes romances such as *A New Beginning* and *Shattered Dreams*.

APPENDIX C: SOME BOOKS BY DAVID BRUCE

Retellings of a Classic Work of Literature

Arden of Faversham: *A Retelling*

Ben Jonson's The Alchemist: *A Retelling*

Ben Jonson's The Arraignment, or Poetaster: *A Retelling*

Ben Jonson's Bartholomew Fair: *A Retelling*

Ben Jonson's The Case is Altered: *A Retelling*

Ben Jonson's Catiline's Conspiracy: *A Retelling*

Ben Jonson's The Devil is an Ass: *A Retelling*

Ben Jonson's Epicene: *A Retelling*

Ben Jonson's Every Man in His Humor: *A Retelling*

Ben Jonson's Every Man Out of His Humor: *A Retelling*

Ben Jonson's The Fountain of Self-Love, or Cynthia's Revels: *A Retelling*

Ben Jonson's The Magnetic Lady, or Humors Reconciled: *A Retelling*

Ben Jonson's The New Inn, or The Light Heart: *A Retelling*

Ben Jonson's Sejanus' Fall: *A Retelling*

Ben Jonson's The Staple of News: *A Retelling*

Ben Jonson's A Tale of a Tub: *A Retelling*

Ben Jonson's Volpone, or the Fox: *A Retelling*

Christopher Marlowe's Complete Plays: Retellings

Christopher Marlowe's Dido, Queen of Carthage: *A Retelling*

Christopher Marlowe's Doctor Faustus: *Retellings of the 1604 A-Text and of the 1616 B-Text*

Christopher Marlowe's Edward II: *A Retelling*

Christopher Marlowe's The Massacre at Paris: *A Retelling*

Christopher Marlowe's The Rich Jew of Malta: *A Retelling*

Christopher Marlowe's Tamburlaine, Parts 1 and 2: *Retellings*

Dante's Divine Comedy: *A Retelling in Prose*

Dante's Inferno: *A Retelling in Prose*

Dante's Purgatory: *A Retelling in Prose*

Dante's Paradise: *A Retelling in Prose*

The Famous Victories of Henry V: *A Retelling*

From the Iliad *to the* Odyssey: *A Retelling in Prose of Quintus of Smyrna's* Posthomerica

George Chapman, Ben Jonson, and John Marston's Eastward Ho! *A Retelling*

George Peele's The Arraignment of Paris: *A Retelling*

George Peele's The Battle of Alcazar: *A Retelling*

George's Peele's David and Bathsheba, and the Tragedy of Absalom: *A Retelling*

George Peele's Edward I: *A Retelling*

George Peele's The Old Wives' Tale: *A Retelling*

George-a-Greene: *A Retelling*
The History of King Leir: *A Retelling*
Homer's Iliad: *A Retelling in Prose*
Homer's Odyssey: *A Retelling in Prose*
J.W. Gent.'s The Valiant Scot: *A Retelling*
Jason and the Argonauts: A Retelling in Prose of Apollonius of Rhodes' Argonautica
John Ford: Eight Plays Translated into Modern English
John Ford's The Broken Heart: *A Retelling*
John Ford's The Fancies, Chaste and Noble: *A Retelling*
John Ford's The Lady's Trial: *A Retelling*
John Ford's The Lover's Melancholy: *A Retelling*
John Ford's Love's Sacrifice: *A Retelling*
John Ford's Perkin Warbeck: *A Retelling*
John Ford's The Queen: *A Retelling*
John Ford's 'Tis Pity She's a Whore: *A Retelling*
John Lyly's Campaspe: *A Retelling*
John Lyly's Endymion, The Man in the Moon: *A Retelling*
John Lyly's Galatea: *A Retelling*
John Lyly's Love's Metamorphosis: *A Retelling*
John Lyly's Midas: *A Retelling*
John Lyly's Mother Bombie: *A Retelling*
John Lyly's Sappho and Phao: *A Retelling*
John Lyly's The Woman in the Moon: *A Retelling*
John Webster's The White Devil: *A Retelling*
King Edward III: *A Retelling*
Mankind: *A Medieval Morality Play* (A Retelling)
Margaret Cavendish's The Unnatural Tragedy: *A Retelling*
The Merry Devil of Edmonton: *A Retelling*
The Summoning of Everyman: *A Medieval Morality Play* (A Retelling)
Robert Greene's Friar Bacon and Friar Bungay: *A Retelling*
The Taming of a Shrew: *A Retelling*
Tarlton's Jests: A Retelling
Thomas Middleton's A Chaste Maid in Cheapside: *A Retelling*
Thomas Middleton's Women Beware Women: *A Retelling*
Thomas Middleton and Thomas Dekker's The Roaring Girl: *A Retelling*
Thomas Middleton and William Rowley's The Changeling: *A Retelling*
The Trojan War and Its Aftermath: Four Ancient Epic Poems
Virgil's Aeneid: *A Retelling in Prose*
William Shakespeare's 5 Late Romances: Retellings in Prose
William Shakespeare's 10 Histories: Retellings in Prose
William Shakespeare's 11 Tragedies: Retellings in Prose
William Shakespeare's 12 Comedies: Retellings in Prose